Published by: GladEye Press
Interior Design by: J.V. Bolkan
Cover Design by: Sharleen Nelson
ISBN-13: 978-1-951289-16-4
Library of Congress Control Number: 2024940900

10 9 8 7 6 5 4 3 2

The body text is presented in Adobe Jenson Pro, 11 point
for easy readability.

Book two of the Risk of Being Ridiculous Trilogy

GUY MAYNARD

Springfield, OR

It was cool to sit around that overcrowded table in the steamy warmth of the union cafeteria, chairs angled every which way to keep squeezing people into our limitlessly expandable circle, Mike and me wolfing down our liberated burgers, the table a mess of coffee and soda cups and overflowing ash trays—to be a part of this laughter and these stories. Cozy and secure with these people, but more than that, connected to them and to whatever it was that all of us together added up to. That was it. This energy, this spirit, this defiance, this joy, this revolution that was only partly political.

This was the core of our cell, our collective, our soviet, our cadre, our guerilla band—this gathering of boys and girls, men and women, who were figuring out how to say no to what stood in the way of lives that made some intrinsic sense to us and yes to whatever might lead us toward that sense.

I wished Sarah was there now, because this was the life behind all the words I spouted, the reality behind all the theories I espoused: kids who should be planning their careers and figuring out how to get their piece of the incredible wealth that was waiting for them instead were trying to figure out how to fight war and racism, how to live decent lives in a world overloaded with valueless wealth and governed by worthless values, as well as trying to figure out how to get stoned that afternoon or to get some desired somebody into their life or their bed. And there were as many answers to try on as there were people at this table—more than that: multiply this table by other tables in this cafeteria and tables like these in Amherst and Champaign and around the world.

Sarah had a place at this table, in this circle, here and now. Then it would make sense to her—that it wasn't just me, but me as part of this whole that she belonged to as sure as shit.

Stu tried to talk us out of it. "Hayakawa? Who the fuck is Hayakawa? Is he worth your time? There's a much better show at the Tea Party tonight. Ten Years After and Mott the Hoople. They've got a much better sound than Hayakawa."

"Sure, Stuie, go have your fun at the rock and roll show," Mike said, a little smile peeking out from his beard. "We'll be out fighting for your rights to get high and enjoy music. Think of us out in the streets while you're in that warm safe concert."

"Oh, Mike," Brian was half-laughing. "What does Hayakawa have to do with getting high and listening to music? That's such bullshit."

"Everything, man," Mike said, lowering his bushy eyebrows. "Hayakawa has everything to do with getting high and listening to music. Am I right, Tucker?"

I laughed. Even though he was just busting their balls, Mike was right in some ways. It was all the same fight. The Chicano and black students at San Francisco State. Rock and roll. The commuter students at Northeastern. Our wall. The working class kids at Boston English. The lies of American history. The Black Panthers. Smoking dope. Lenny splitting his time between the Coast Guard and our couch. The GE strikers and our friends who got busted in demonstrations supporting them. The bullshit of the American Dream. The Vietnam War. Little Eddie escaping. Making love not war. Luke underground. The girls at 858. The GIs used by the government. The injunction against me. The draft. Television and art. Sarah and me trying to figure how to love in the middle of all this shit. Peace and love and revolution. Hayakawa and Ten Years After and Mott the Hoople. All one great big bundle—and we all knew that in our own way. We'd had this discussion a million times coming at it from a million different angles and we weren't going to get any closer to saying it the same way on this night as Mike and Patrick and I waited for the guys from Myles Standish—Jerry, Wes, and Mac—before heading out to the demonstration at Northeastern. We'd do our demonstrating and Stu and Brian would go to their show and Lenny would nurse his trusty six-pack, then we'd all meet back at Mountfort Street and get high and tell each other about what we'd done. And we'd never really know who'd changed what.

"Yeah, man, you're absolutely right," I said. "I heard the first thing Hayakawa did at San Francisco State was ban rock and roll and crack down on pot smoking. Then he went after the militant third-world students." I grinned at Brian, then Stu, who shook his head with a smile. He knew we were going to Northeastern no matter what he said.

This little exchange loosened me up a bit. I was feeling kind of uptight. The Myles boys were late. I was going to miss my phone call to Sarah tonight. She was going out to dinner with her family to celebrate her father's birthday. Sure as hell she would have tried to talk me out of going to Northeastern.

I did have mixed feelings about going, but I knew that we had to go. We had to show the pigs that the crackdown at BU, the injunctions they were getting all over town—the Northeastern administration had a court order to try stop tonight's action (I wasn't named in that one)—the repression of the Panthers, and the crazy-ass conspiracy trial going on in Chicago weren't going to crush the Movement. The truth was, the pigs' tactics were working. As the stakes were raised, fewer and fewer people were showing up for demonstrations, and militants were more and more isolated. I knew that we had to keep fighting, but sometimes I just wasn't sure what the Movement was anymore, exactly where it was moving us to. I couldn't really make sense of it in a way that went beyond this one decision in front of me, beyond this night and whatever was waiting for us at Northeastern. But somehow it made even less sense to me to not go, to join Stu and Brian at the Tea Party. I knew that would please Sarah, but not going to Northeastern was a kind of surrender that I wasn't ready to make.

TRIAL

A Long Year from Here to There

Eastward I go only by force; but westward
I go free. I must walk to Oregon ...
—Henry David Thoreau

We eased into lovemaking. Kisses, and soft touches, and gentle strokes. So much had changed since the stumbling, hungry, glorious passion of the year before. Shit had gotten serious in spite of all our efforts to deny and defy it. Now, we made a serious kind of love, slow and deliberate, tender and considered, conscious of the magnitude of this moment, savoring, cherishing, holding on to the blossoming euphoria as long as we possibly could. It was almost a sad kind of love, but as magnificent as any we'd ever experienced.

February 2, 1970 [Boston]

It was surprisingly warm when my father and I crossed the bridge over the turnpike toward Kenmore Square. A light rain was falling. I wore the blue knit hat Sarah had given me to hide my hair. My father didn't have a hat so we walked fast, though the rain didn't seem to bother him much as we grasped for ways to get into the conversation we both knew we had to have.

"When did you get to Boston?" I asked.

"Very late last night," he said. "Took a cab to Aunt Ruby's." He looked down toward me, smiling uneasily. "No school?"

"No. Well, yeah, I have classes but I couldn't handle it today."

"I guess I can understand that," he said. "I'm glad you were home. I wish you had a phone."

"I know. Sorry. It would have been a hassle trying to find me at school."

We were heading toward Sizzlebord, a sort of fast-food delicatessen, where we could sit and eat lunch—and talk. It was close and easy and I guess the food was all right. Mostly I knew Sizzlebord because when Mike and Stu and I (and Jeffrey and Walter at different times) worked as after-hour janitors at the Shawmut Bank next door, we'd dump our trash in the Sizzlebord dumpster because it was closer than the one we were supposed to use. As we smoked joints in the bank president's office after we finished the work of our three-hour shift in an hour, we'd do a riff of how we would respond if we ever got caught filling up the wrong dumpster. "Seezel Board?" we'd say in some vaguely eastern European accent. "Vat eees Seezel Board? No understand Seezel Board. No understand Angleees." We never did get caught and get the chance to try out our bit, but we did get fired from that job for reasons never explained to us.

My father and I entered the brightly lit, shiny clean Sizzlebord, found a table and ordered hot pastrami and cheese sandwiches that were soulless but quick.

"So tell me where things stand," my father finally said, the ridge of wrinkles across his long forehead tightening. It had been four days since I was arrested. I'd called my parents in Illinois after my arraignment, when things got really strange, but I was fried and they were freaked out, so it was not a particularly productive conversation.

"I need a lawyer, that's the first thing, I guess. Maybe we can call Harry Stone after this." Harry was a Movement lawyer who had represented a bunch of us students who faced disciplinary hearings after the takeover of a dean's office at Boston University and was now helping me fight an injunction that BU had filed against me and a few other activists. A Lawyer's Guild lawyer had handled my arraignment—a little clumsily—but now I needed my own lawyer.

"I know you like Harry Stone, but your Uncle Sean thinks you need a better lawyer to deal with this situation." He tried to say that as calmly as he could, knowing I wouldn't like it. But I wasn't looking for a fight, either. I knew this was serious shit and my uncle was well connected in Boston legal circles. I also knew that my father really was trying to help me. Shit, I was charged with assaulting a police officer with a deadly weapon and my father's reaction from the start had been concerned and supportive. Through my teenage years, he and I had staked positions on the length of my hair, the war in Vietnam, taking out the garbage, school, his drinking, racism, cleaning my room, Richard Nixon, using the family Corvair, the draft—basically any issue or interaction that came up between us—and dug in for an extended battle from which neither of us would ever surrender. But now we were just a father and a son, a loving father and a son in some deep trouble. All that fiery rhetoric we'd thrown at each other seemed like artifacts of a silly game we'd played in another lifetime. He even looked different. It'd been so long since I'd seen him as anything other than a foil, the living example of everything I didn't want to be. Now, I could see a tenderness in his soft blue eyes, streaked with red from days of worry and the stress of travel. I must have seen that warmth before but it struck me as unfamiliar and a little unnerving. He'd even let his close-cropped curly brown hair, which formed a distinct M across his brow, stretch out just a bit.

"That may be true," I said, though I did really like Harry and was scared of where my uncle's direction might take us. "But I'd like to at least talk to Harry, get his thoughts. We need to talk about how this affects the injunction and that kind of stuff. I think Harry is at least a good place to start."

He agreed with that. Wow. Five minutes in and we'd listened to each other and agreed to a middle ground approach to our first step. Neither of us said anything for a while. The noise of the busy restaurant seemed to swell around us. I wolfed down my sandwich and wished I'd ordered two. Turns out the lawyer part was sort of easy, a detail, no real decision had been made. He finished his sandwich and seemed to scrutinize me, forcing a grin to set up his next question.

"So . . . what happened that night?" he asked. "We were so concerned about you and all the details of the arraignment were so confusing that I still don't have a clear picture of what happened. Can you fill me in?"

"Sure, sure," I said as I tried to figure out where to start, how much to say.

I told him that Mike, Patrick, Jerry, and a couple other guys and I had decided to go to the demonstration at Northeastern to protest a speech by S.I. Hayakawa, who had repressed a student anti-racism movement when he was president of San Francisco State University. We weren't expecting it to be a militant or big protest, even though we knew a group of the Weathermen would be there—they had even asked us to join them; we had said, maybe, we'll see. I said I wasn't sure why we went, except the Movement had been in decline, fewer and fewer people showing up for protests. I think we just wanted to be there, to show that there was still an active citywide Movement in Boston. Nobody, except maybe the Weathermen, expected a big fight.

But the cops and the Northeastern authorities blew up what probably would have been a small, noisy but nonviolent protest into a riot scene by turning away people who had legitimate tickets to Hayakawa's speech but didn't have a Northeastern ID. They had sold tickets (at double the price) to people without that ID but they wouldn't let them in. Even worse, "suspicious" people (long-haired or Black) with tickets and the right IDs, weren't allowed in and had their IDs confiscated. The people they did let in had to have their pictures taken and their seat numbers written down next to their names. The authorities had let their fear of disruption force them into actions that ensured an even more dramatic disruption. By the time our little group arrived in the quadrangle outside the auditorium where Hayakawa was going to speak, the crowd had swelled from a small group of militants to a mass of 1,000 or more.

I paused to take a sip of Coke. My father had a little notebook where he jotted something down every now and then, but he was listening intently, not interrupting me. In the old world, when we were on opposite sides, he would have challenged half a dozen of the things I'd already said. But he just listened—and, I think, believed me.

I told him the situation was explosive when we arrived. Police lining the steps up to the auditorium, the angry surging crowd pushed up against them. Like us, the cops were not expecting a major confrontation. These were event management cops, not riot cops. We made our way up to the base of the steps. We saw some folks we knew from the Movement, but most of the throng was either pissed-off people who had been denied admission or curious Northeastern students, attracted by the intense energy engulfing their usually placid quadrangle. One Movement friend, a BU student leader, was actively trying to keep people calm. The dozen or so Weathermen, who we found at the base of the steps screaming at the cops, were doing the opposite, trying to stir up the anger, provoke a fight.

My father winced when I mentioned the Weathermen for the second time. His mind had not opened enough to accept that I hung around with Weathermen.

I told him we had a brief shouted meeting with the Weathermen and our friend who was trying to keep things peaceful. Our group of six decided this was not a good place or situation to pick a fight with cops. The inexperienced would panic and scatter as soon as the police attacked, some of them would get hurt and those of us known to the Boston police could be easily picked off by the undercover Red Squad we knew was circulating among the protestors. It was a tricky position, I told him, we liked seeing so many people so angry at the cops and at the school administration. It was an opportunity to radicalize a whole bunch of people, so we wanted to encourage the anger and the chanting, the fists raised in the air, the solidarity of standing up to the pigs, but we wanted it to stop short of a riot.

But the anger was bigger than our strategy could contain. While we were talking with the Weathermen, the cops had been reinforced by the Tactical Police Force, riot cops with their bigger sticks and vicious swagger, but they too were underequipped—no helmets or shields. After some kid knocked a cop's hat off, the police cleared the steps, pushing the crowd back, adding another layer of intensity to the crowd's fury. Rocks and maybe even bricks crashed against the building. I saw one kid standing above me on a bench throw something—I couldn't see what—toward the police line, followed by the sound of glass breaking. "Hey, man," I yelled at the kid, "you've gotta cool it."

I felt my adrenaline surging as I got deeper into my story, already longer than I intended. But how could I just tell him about the few minutes around my arrest. It didn't make sense, just as an isolated event. I took another sip of my Coke and a deep breath. He stared at me, his eyes now wide and anxious.

"But he couldn't hear me. The crowd cheered and he looked in my direction with a big smile on his face. I had no time to react to him as people in front starting pushing at me. The cops had attacked, waded into the crowd. I tried to find Mike and Patrick and Jerry and the other guys. Only Patrick was nearby. We got together and tried to calm people down. 'Slow down, stick together,' we yelled. I could hear our other friends shouting similar things. But people panicked and were trying to get away as fast as they could. I looked back and saw the police line closing in on us, so Patrick and I picked up our pace, heading toward the street as the crowd thinned out around us. I looked back again, saw a tall thin girl in a dark blue pea coat fall down as she tried to get away from the advancing cops. Two cops immediately started beating her with their billy clubs. Blood spurted from her head, staining her stringy brown hair—and they kept hitting her.

I went back toward them and yelled at the cops to stop but they kept beating her as others cops passed them and started coming toward me. Patrick grabbed me, told me I couldn't help her, and that we had to get out of there.

"I was so pissed, Dad, so pissed and ashamed that I couldn't stop them. It was like I got a shot of some super power juice. Patrick and I leaped over the fence between the quadrangle and the street, moving to join the small remaining crowd of protestors who had stopped just on the other side of the trolley tracks that ran down the middle of Huntington Avenue. We both picked up rocks from around the trolley tracks . . ." Now a grimace creased his face. ". . . and stopped when we were in the middle of the crowd to look for our friends. But we still couldn't find them. The cops had reformed their line across the street from us, maybe a hundred of them, and they started marching toward us with their batons up against their chest just aching to beat a few more kids. They knocked down some kid waiting for the train and kicked him as they passed. Kid wasn't even with us, just waiting for the train. And they kept coming toward us. All I saw was this mass of blue violence—Pigs!

They really were, Dad. If you could have seen the look on their faces . . . I was pissed. I was ashamed. I was tired of running, and I threw that rock into that line of cops . . ."

I took another long deep breath as the heated fleshy smell of that scene suddenly filled my head.

" . . . and then I felt somebody grab me, a tall Black guy, and I pushed his hand away and I ran into the crowd away from the cops. I saw Mike and Jerry and yelled at them that a cop was after me but they couldn't react fast enough and all of sudden it was just me and the cop—I'm sure he was a cop—maybe ten or fifteen feet behind me, out of the crowd. I turned down an alley, sure I could outrun him, but I hadn't gotten very far when he yelled, 'Stop or I'll shoot' … I stopped."

My father looked stunned. His whole body seemed to flinch. I looked away from him, around the restaurant, heard the buzz surrounding us again, felt the too-bright lights of Sizzlebord pounding down on me, wondered if anybody had been listening to my narration. Nobody seemed to be paying any attention to us.

"Do you know what happened to the rock you threw?" he finally asked. "Did you hit anybody?"

"I don't know." That was a lie. That part of the scene always ends with the cop's hat falling off as he recoiled from the rock hitting his right cheek, him going to his knees, blood trickling down his face as his brother cops surrounded him. And I felt righteous and good for the split second before the chase began. "Maybe. That guy grabbed me so fast, I never saw where it went. But I know it wasn't a brick and I know I didn't hit Fletcher Riley." The last part was the truth.

At my arraignment, the day after I was arrested, I was accused of throwing a brick that struck a Black policeman, Fletcher Riley, while he stood on the steps of the auditorium where Hayakawa was about to speak—before the cops charged the crowd, while I was still trying to keep things from escalating. That charge was a lie. I hit some White cop in the street with a rock that fit comfortably in my hand. They'd charged me with hitting the wrong cop. I was innocent—of that. So, that made my lie irrelevant. I admitted to throwing something. And no one could ever prove whether I saw what happened to that rock. Why should I give my father more to worry about?

"Dad, you know what a weak arm I have. I'm a second baseman. Do you think I could throw a brick as far as they say I did with anything on it?"

He did crack a bit of a smile. In Little League, when he was my biggest fan, I'd cost my team a championship by making a feeble—and late—throw to first on a routine grounder. That hadn't been funny at the time, but now our shared knowledge of my weak arm helped ease the tension some.

But the thing was Fletcher Riley was the headline injured cop of the dozen or so who got hurt in the riot. His mouth was smashed. His jaw was screwed up. He was all wired up so he couldn't talk during my arraignment, having to nod to indicate answers. My bail was the highest of the twenty-eight people facing charges. I may have been innocent, but I was the one they'd picked to be the baddest of the bad guys in this thing and we already had plenty of proof that the cops wouldn't hesitate to lie. While I was in jail awaiting bail the night I was arrested, a Lawyer's Guild attorney who was there to try to get us out overheard this conversation: Cop A: We got the faggot here who hit Riley with a brick. Cop B: Did you get the brick? Cop A: No. Cop B: Then you better go get one.

My father and I sat in Sizzlebord for a couple of hours as the unseasonably warm drizzle steamed the windows, casting Kenmore Square in a surreal light, gray and dripping and blurry. We went through the details of my night in jail and the arraignment, talked about some photographs my sister Cary was trying to find that apparently showed Fetcher Riley on the police lines long after he had supposedly been hit. Was anything true? We talked about my school—how I had to keep at it though it seemed wildly irrelevant now—and the injunction. Before my arrest, BU had named me in an injunction against eight activists—mostly dogmatic communists; I was more of a hippie communist—using bizarre circumstantial facts to link me to them. We talked about my mother and other sisters in Illinois, how they were handling it. We talked about sweet Sarah and my roommates, their amazing support, and the door-to-door dorm fundraising that had raised my bail. It was a terrible situation. I faced serious jail time. My father, not in great financial shape, was trying to figure out how he could come up with the money to hire the kind of lawyer I was going to need.

This was a conversation neither of us ever wanted or expected, though in some ways the dynamic of our relationship over the past four or five years had been moving us inexorably toward it. It was hard but it was kind of wonderful, too, a new start for us.

We called Harry and arranged to meet with him later that afternoon in his cluttered office at his small home in Brookline. After expressing his concern for me, the first thing he told us was that my case was more than he could handle, that I needed a better, more experienced lawyer. He suggested a guy named William Bowman, a prominent attorney known for defending civil rights and other activists, including my Weathermen friend Luke, who was now doing two years in Walpole State Prison for assaulting office workers at a Harvard think tank. My father took down all the information but I knew he was reluctant to work with anybody in any way associated with the Movement. My uncle had suggested a member of the Anglo/Irish/Italian establishment in Boston, John Orsini. He was kind of famous, even appeared regularly on some public television show. But he was a lot more expensive than Bowman, a $2,500 retainer rather than the $1,000 we had heard Bowman charged. After we left Harry's, I argued some for Bowman, but I knew it was an argument I would probably lose. My parents were paying for it and my uncle was in the thick of the Boston legal scene so his advice was worth a lot. And the truth was, I was scared shitless.

March 13, 1970 [Boston]

Dear Family,

It's been awhile since I've sat down and wrote you a good letter. I'm sick now and in bed so I have some time. I don't think it's anything very serious, but I feel pretty miserable. I have a cold and a fever, about 100.6 last night. I went to the BU clinic today and they gave me some penicillan (sp?) and a prescription for this other stuff Drioxil or something like that. Sarah was here to take care of me but she left tonight and my brothers Mike and Stu have taken her place. I missed a midterm in science today. I will have to make it up I guess.

I received the copy of your letter asking for character references yesterday. It's good and flattering. My only objection is the use of the word "bystander"—there's really no such thing as an innocent bystander anymore. But that, I suppose, is minor. I really appreciate all you are doing, honest, and if sometimes I seem unenthusiastic and negative its only because this whole situation is negative—the only victory is not losing. It's a defensive battle—there's no way we can smash the state, we can only stop them from smashing us.

I talked to the shrink again. First I recited, for the 4000th time, the story of what happened at NE Jan. 29. Then he raised the question of my plea. He gave me the impression that he thinks I have a better chance of not going to jail if I plead guilty and say that it was due to emotional problems in me and that I would receive treatment for these. He raised the question because, depending on the plea, he has to approach this in different ways. If I plead not guilty then he would say—if his findings bear this out—that I'm a nonviolent person. If I plead guilty then he has to say that I have tendencies to be violent because of flaws in my character which can be corrected. He presented them ostensibly as equal alternatives, but he seemed to favor the latter. This isn't based on his psychiatric findings but on how he perceives my legal case. I'm going to talk to Zinzer—Orsini's assistant who I've been meeting with—about it. I'm pretty sure that I much prefer pleading not guilty. First of all because I am—even though the destination of my rock isn't certain and the fact that the grand jury charged me with a second count doesn't help—like Goebbels said, the way to convince people of a lie is to tell a bigger lie. Secondly, because I don't think that my actions were due to flaws in my character or emotional problems, but rather an irrational—yet pretty human—response to the grotesque brutality of the police. It is they who are insane and vicious and, in fact, they should be on trial. But is it an emotional problem to be outraged by brutality— outraged to the point of grasping for any way to try to stop it? I don't think so. Violence is such an ill-used concept. Everybody's horrified that students burned down a bank in Santa Barbara—yet accept passively the incredible violence the gov't of the US is responsible for all over the world. The YAF condemn student "violence" and yet say that we should bomb Hanoi. I guess people can accept violence as long as it doesn't get too close to home, as long as it's only on TV or in the newspaper.

School grows more irrelevant by the day. They are hassling me about attendance now. I wish it was over. I wish I could drop out now but I don't s'pose that would look good in court. Yesterday I went to my poetry class and we talked about a lot of stuff—mostly how does one survive in this insane society. No answers—even Dr. Barrington feels an emptiness in his life—he is very regretful about getting caught up in the academic game and is still looking for a way out. I've really tried to get back into school—but it's so much bullshit it's incredible (sorry if I offend you but that's the only word that says it right). I've been doing a lot more reading and writing but little of it has to do with school.

Sarah had been here since Sunday. I was sick most of the time, which was a drag but it was nice to have her here to take care of me. She made me go to the clinic today.

She went to some of my classes with me, including poetry which was the only one she was impressed by. We made some candles yesterday which was fun. I feel sad now that she has gone—but a good kind of sadness—that comes from happiness—if you know what I mean. Somebody came up to us in the Union today and said they heard we were getting married in April. That's pretty funny. Since I got arrested I've been the subject of many campus rumors—a pretty dubious honor. We're not getting married in April by the way or anytime in the foreseeable future. We had fun playing with the idea—I decided I'd have to have five best men—Scott, Alexander, Barry, Stu, and Mike. Mike insisted that he be the head best man. Eddie (the escapee from the nut house) wanted to be the head usher and hand out joints to all the guests. Anyway it ain't gonna happen for a while anyway—I can't imagine being married.

My spirits are all right. I haven't got a lot done this past week between being sick and Sarah being here and going to classes. I have sort of repressed the threat of going to jail—it seems pointless spending many hours worrying about it. I figure that what has to be done is to strive to develop myself—with the people around me—to a point where there is no way we can lose. If we can build something positive and beautiful inside then no matter what the state does we will survive and go forward.

One of the pills I took is making me groggy and I must sleep. I will write more tomorrow.

Hello. I got your letter, Dad, today. Answers to your questions. 1) I haven't got a job because I've been sick. I've got a good prospect for a file clerk job at the Lahey Clinic that I will check out tomorrow. 2) I'm unclear as to the status of the injunction and will ask Zinzer next time we talk, next week. 3) Yes, I need money—would like to buy some sneakers if that's OK. I'm pretty low on footgear. 4) I haven't talked to Uncle Sean mainly because I've had nothing to discuss with him and I'm very poor at making idle conversation. I realize that he has helped me an awful lot and I'm very appreciative—but there is still a cultural chasm between us which makes communication difficult. Please remember that my culture is important to me and that while I'm willing to view a person in terms of where he's coming from, I expect, at least, a little of the same, which means that long hair, rock and roll, communal living and sharing, developing real relationships with people not based on games and facades, living in pursuit of joy, etc. etc. are not just phases I'm going thru but that is my life and I only ask people to recognize that. That doesn't just go for Sean but for most adults. Do you see what I mean? I'm a person. I'm real and how I live is real, it's not just a dream. OK. I don't mean to sound aloof—that's not the right word—but that's how I feel. 5) Brooding? I don't know. I don't feel sorry for myself too much. I don't relive the scene over and over anymore. I'm more and more concerned about building positive things—trying to figure out where to go from here. A phase of my life ended Jan. 29 and now I'm trying to make sense out of the new one. I brood over that I guess. 6) You have been so good and done so much already, just please don't commit to things without checking with me.

Well, that's about it—for now—from this end. I love you all very much and appreciate everything. I will write again soon.

Love,
Ben

May 5–8, 1970 [Boston]

Sirens ripped through deserted Kenmore Square. The chants and cheers of bands of marauding kids echoed in the distance down Commonwealth Avenue. The streets were a battle zone and I was an involuntary noncombatant. I couldn't make the four-block walk home without crossing through territory occupied by the Boston Tactical Police Force, so I was holed up in the lobby of the Myles Standish dorm, smoking and scribbling out a poem, waiting for daylight and the cover of the morning crowds to get back to my apartment and then get the hell out of town.

The National Guard had killed four kids the day before at Kent State University in Ohio. A demonstration scheduled for this day at Boston Common to protest Nixon's invasion of Cambodia—the same event the Kent State kids were protesting—had become huge after the news from Ohio. Fucking Nixon had the nerve to say, "When dissent turns to violence it invites tragedy." The kids tossed a few rocks at the soldiers and they opened fire. When the government turns its weapons on its own people it invites revolution. More than 25,000 people showed up at the Common—Mike and Stu and Dale and Patrick and I and a bunch of other friends went down there. And when all the outraged speeches and clenched-fist chanting were done, a lot of kids took to the streets—disrupting traffic, breaking a few windows here and there, urging onlookers to join them—from the Common up Commonwealth toward BU, across the Mass Ave bridge toward MIT and Harvard, all over the student sections of the city.

Of course, I couldn't go in the streets. It was a risk just going to the mass rally, but we stayed in the middle of the crowd, my friends sort of surrounding me. Mike, Stu, and Patrick rode the subway back with me to Kenmore, then Mike and Patrick took off to find the action, Stu went back to Mountfort Street, and I stopped in to see some friends at Myles Standish, to say goodbye. It was my last night in Boston, at least for a while.

We smoked some pot and I took a hit of some mescaline that turned out to be an easy smooth psychedelic high—blue and wavy with just enough push to keep me floating above the weariness and wariness of the last few days of school, of the last few months of insanity in my life, and of the intense reaction that had spread among us as we grokked the reality that the government was willing to kill White kids now, along with Black militants and millions of Vietnamese.

But I was having a good time with the kids at Myles who I'd spent two intense years with, telling stories, shouted above the loud music that rocked the second floor dorm room, when the street fight hit Kenmore. First, we saw forty or fifty kids running into the square, pounding on cars stalled by the sudden congestion, yelling and chanting, the sound of shattered glass bringing ringing cheers and louder chants. Pretty sure they smashed the windows of Sizzlebord. Not far behind were clusters of Boston Police paddy wagons, lights blazing, sirens screaming, coming up Commonwealth and down Beacon Street. But the clogged traffic slowed them down and the kids, swelled by new recruits from the square, ran wild and free down the center of Comm Ave toward the heart of BU, where more would undoubtedly join in.

It was hard watching all this from a second-floor window. Man, I wanted to be out there with them. I saw Mike in the middle of the crowd, but ... That was one of the reasons I knew

I had to get out of Boston. I wasn't in jail, but I was not a free man.

Eventually, my Myles friends started fading but I was still wired from some combination of the adrenaline of the day and the mescaline of the evening. I left their room intending to go home—one last night at Mountfort Street—but when I got to the front door of the dorm, leading out to the street, I saw a stack of cop cars in the middle of Kenmore Square and a phalanx of riot ready TPF cops milling around them—maybe some of the motherfuckers who came to my cell the night of my arrest to tell me exactly how many ways they would fuck me up if they ever saw me on the street. I wasn't going out there any time soon.

I curled up with a pen and a notebook on one of the cushy couches in the Myles lobby. It was sometime after midnight and nobody was coming in or going out. Just me and my mescaline-tinged thoughts in the quiet lobby, scratching out a eulogy to my time in Boston. Two years, almost. I was so earnest and scared when my uncle dropped me off at West Campus twenty months earlier. A college kid all of a sudden. Didn't know anybody else. I'd left my rock and roll band, friends I would have died for, a town I had begrudgingly come to know and love in Champaign-Urbana. For what? To make some mark on the world. To be an intellectual. To be something like who I thought I was supposed to be. And, OK, yeah, to play hard in the culture being built around drugs and rock and roll, to find some kind of love, to be a campus radical in a place where it mattered: Boston. All that was part of it, but I was mostly a scared kid entering an unknown world trying to find a future. And how different was this scared kid hiding in a dorm lobby from that kid first entering a dorm at the other end of campus? The intellectual thing had worked for a while. First two terms on the dean's list, but that soon got lost in smoke and outrage and the pursuit of Sarah. I'd made a whole new set of friends that I would die for—and who would die for me, or at least bail me out of jail and try to keep me safe. We raised plenty of hell from the dean's office to the streets of Washington, DC. We lit up our dorms and apartments and all places in between with sweet smoke and outrageous music. We tripped to unimaginable places, decaying and dark, glorious and infinite.

And love … man, I'd found love. Found an impossible love. Had my heart twisted every which way, broken into little pieces. What I wanted could never happen—but it did. It pulsed and surged through me, this life-giving force, a powerful antidote to the bullying madness of dreary classrooms and cold-blooded courtrooms and the ruthless soulless tyranny of the lives us White middle-class kids were supposed to lead.

But now what? No more school. No more Mountfort Street.

The next week or so was mapped out, a road trip with Mike and Sarah. But then … a big blank unknown. Summer? The trial, all the more frightening now because the second assault charge they indicted me on was probably the one I actually did? Sarah and me? The rest of the Boston tribe? Champaign? Sarah's Philadelphia? Boston? The wonderful imagined West, where we all wanted to end up, where none of us had ever been? How would we get there? What would we do? Just where exactly would we go? No fucking idea.

When I had wandered—alone, earnest, and frightened—into the buzz of the West Campus lobby in September 1968, it was into a deep unknown, but that uncertainty had a structure to it: a room to sleep where I was forced to connect to other people, places I was supposed to be most days, breakfast, lunch and dinner every day but Sunday. You could trip your brains out watching the Jefferson Airplane or yell at Spiro Agnew until the cops chased you away or watch the sun come up over the Public Gardens and you always had somewhere to stagger back to. Even after the dorms, in the now ending days of Mountfort Street and other friends' apartments, there was a web of places, friends and friends of friends, where we could land after almost anything.

But, this unknown that lay beyond the barrier of cops between me and my final exit from Mountfort Street, was as big as the US of A, from California to the New York island, as amorphous as freedom, as inscrutable as love.

Soft light was beginning to crack through the darkness. Kenmore Square started to come to life. I got up and stretched and looked out the door, still saw a few TPF cops, in silhouette, the glow of their cigarettes punching through the slowly yielding gray.

> good bye boston
> i've run and played and stormed
> through your streets enough
> so many tomorrows have come and gone
> so many dreams
> so many answers
> so many perfect plans
>
> I don't know
> I don't know
> I don't know
> About tomorrow
> Or much of anything for sure
> Only that it will come
> And we will be glad

good bye boston
we only have a few hours left
i've hated and loved you
run away to come here and run away to go
i found love and a lonely jail cell
in leaving, ambivalence surrounds me

good bye boston
it's been a gas
but today is the tomorrow
we thought would never come
i can't miss your steel
or your sirens
or the death in the eyes of your masses
but I will miss
the faces of the tribe

we can never lose each other
because we found ourselves in each other
and we gotta keep going
not on the memory
but with that new life we feel growing inside.

We are everything they say we are—and more.

On strike!

I was scared of the TPF cops. I was scared that I would end
up in prison. I was still scared that I couldn't hold Sarah's love.

But I wasn't scared of the gaping unknown in front of me. I just wanted to leap, eyes fully open and my arms wide ready to caress it.

[Oxford, Ohio]

It took us a while to get Mike out of jail. It took us a while just to find him. Sarah and I had slept in her friend Sally's dorm room at Western College for Women, but Mike was still flying from some dex he'd taken on the trip from Philly to Oxford, Ohio, so he decided to roam the campuses of Western and nearby Miami University while we slept. It was a bad night to do that.

After I'd finally made my way back to Mountfort Street, Mike and I said goodbye to Stu and Herschel, pledged to see them somewhere, some time—and hit the road as soon as we could with a friend of Sarah's who'd been staying with us. We were going to meet up with Sarah in Philly to head west to take a car to her brother Harry, who was in medical school in Kansas City. Sarah's folks thought she was driving with Sally's roommate to Oxford. Then, the story went, Sally and Sarah would continue on to Kansas City and they would fly home to Philly from there. Sarah's parents had grudgingly acknowledged our relationship. I was allowed in their house and they would pass on my phone messages. But they still weren't quite ready for her to take a cross-country road trip with me.

BU was on strike when we left, and the school essentially shut down like other schools across Boston and the country. This was serious shit. Though I made it safely from Myles to Mountfort Street, the whole area surrounding BU still felt like a war zone and that sense followed us all the way to Philly and on to Oxford. We were the enemy, traveling through territory controlled by the pigs. And we—conveniently for them—were easily identifiable. My hair hung down past my shoulders, blond and ragged, like straw tossed in the wind. Sarah's once-straightened chestnut brown hair was now wild and free, winding lushly down to drape over her shoulders. And Mike, man, he was the freakiest of us all. A mass of bark-like reddish-brown hair surrounded the bushy beard and thick glasses over sunken eyes that dominated his face. And he was big and burly, a mean defensive lineman in high school. And oh, yeah, just in case you weren't sure he was a freak's freak, his sneakers left no doubt: he'd written in black magic marker on the white toe caps. "Fuck" on the right, "You" on the left.

So, we could understand that the Oxford Police, investigating a firebomb thrown into Roudebush Hall—the main administration building at Miami University—on the night after the night after Kent State (250 miles away in another corner of Ohio), would find Mike—wide-eyed from the speed, wandering around campus in the middle of the night—somewhat suspicious.

When he didn't show up at the dorm in the morning, we eventually decided to check at the city jail. And there he was, in a small cell we could see from the front desk, looking groggy from a night of speeding followed by no sleep and especially scary because the cops had taken his glasses away, leaving him looking like a big old mole who's just crawled out of his hole. But the cops didn't know what to do with him. If they decided to charge him with something, they had to transfer him to the Butler County jail down in Hamilton. They didn't have any evidence. He really hadn't done anything. But he sure looked guilty to those small-town Ohio cops. Somehow between Sarah, Sally, and me, we convinced the cops to let him go. We told them we were just there overnight. He couldn't sleep in the girls' dorm (though we didn't quite explain how I did), so he just decided to walk around till we left in the morning. We knew he looked like somebody who would firebomb an administration building, but he really didn't have anything to do with it (we were pretty sure). And we promised to get out of town as soon as they released him.

[Champaign-Urbana, Illinois]

I-74 from Indianapolis into Champaign-Urbana was a memory lane for me. I'd traveled that route so many times with the band and on the many runs between the East Coast and Illinois in the last few years. One trip after a late gig in Bloomington, Indiana, I was driving the red Chevy wagon and everybody else was asleep by the time I turned west on that interstate in Indianapolis— and I was tired. It's a straight flat shot and I did that 100 miles to Champaign in exactly one hour. Just put the pedal down until the speedometer reached 100 and kept it there. I was like a machine in a dream, flying past the Crawfordsville lights and Covington and Danville in the desolate hours of the morning.

But now it was a creamy blue early May afternoon and we were deep in hostile territory, so I stuck right at 70 as we closed in on my old hometown. It was cool to have Sarah and Mike with me. They'd met some of my Illinois friends—Barry and Scotty and a few others—but they'd never been to Champaign. We were just going to spend a night and then head to Kansas City the next day. But they'd meet my parents—I was anxious for my parents to meet Sarah, to see what an amazing woman I'd somehow coaxed into hanging out with me, and Mike was always good with parents because he made my rebellion look tame by comparison.

We took the Lincoln Street exit off I-74. We were going to head straight to 501, where Scott and Alexander and a bunch of other freaks lived, before going to my parents' house. Man, what a trip cruising toward campus with Sarah and Mike, over the streets of my high school years, such a foreign time now, but the houses and the streetlights and the sidewalks and trees and the corner shops and those black fertile spring Illinois smells were all the same. It was me that was foreign now.

We turned right on Green, the main campus thoroughfare, and saw a commotion up ahead. The streets were full of people. We pulled over and parked and walked toward the Illini Union. No way to get through otherwise. The crowd was building and chanting. On Green Street? At the University of Illinois? Not even three years ago, about fifty of us, mostly UI students but also a few high school students, like me, had walked from the Union up Green Street to the Selective Service office to protest the war and the draft. We walked on the sidewalk because we couldn't get a permit to march on the streets. We were harassed and heckled and splashed with water as cars ran through big puddles to spray us. Now, there were hundreds, maybe even thousands, of kids filling Green Street, chanting "Strike! Strike! Strike!" throwing their fists in the air. Scanning the crowd looking for anybody we knew, we suddenly caught sight of a line of National Guard formed along the lawn in front of the Illini Union, weapons raised across their chest. Holy shit, man, we really were at war.

We eventually found Scott and Alexander, hanging out in front of Deluxe Billiards, a block and a half from the Union, bottles of Falstaff in hand, watching the intense street scene with amused curiosity. When he caught sight of me, Scott raised his arched eyebrow and said, "Hell, Tucker, should have known you'd show up when the protesting shit was hitting the fan. You're just in time. Is that a coincidence?" We laughed and hugged. Scott smiled approvingly at Sarah, as I introduced them, and Mike and Alexander were already engaged in a heavy rap about all the craziness everywhere. It was cool to see the different branches of my freak family blend together so naturally. Later, after we'd decided not to join the developing street battle, the same was true with my blood family, as everyone loved Sarah and were kind of dazzled by Mike's unabashed outrageousness.

May 25, 1970 [Erie, Pennsylvania]

"**C**an you tell me what the world's going to look like after your revolution? Can you draw me a picture of the organizational structure?" My father was maybe half serious, but he was at least half drunk, too, so whatever portion of him was serious was also proportionately distorted.

I laughed. "No, I don't think I can draw you a picture." He smiled as though he had scored a point. "I could tell you my fantasy, but I'm not sure that would get at what you want. We're kinda figuring it out as we go, that's the point really."

We were in the Holiday Inn in Erie, Pennsylvania. We were heading to Boston to meet with Orsini and Zinzer to discuss the trial. The court date hadn't been set yet but it could be as soon as late June, so we wanted to make sure we were ready. I'd only been in Champaign-Urbana a couple of weeks after Sarah flew back to Philly once we'd delivered the car to her brother. But I felt like I was treading water there. Waiting for news of the trial. Trying to figure out what was happening with Sarah and me. Mike had gotten deep into the Champaign scene, living with my old friends at 501, while I stayed at my parents' house. I hung out with my friends a lot but my head was someplace else most of the time. Lately, it seemed like Mike was constantly hitting me up for money or food and that was starting to get on my nerves. Mike was my brother through and through but he could be a pain in the ass.

Sarah's brother had told their parents who her traveling companions were on the trip to Kansas City: me and Mike, not her friend Sally. I had this amazing power that forced sweet, innocent Sarah to do bad things. So we—mostly me—were on her parents' shit list again. And she seemed to be yielding to their pressure again. Shit, I thought we were past that by now.

Our big plan was to try to get some money together and head to the West Coast and connect with Mike and Stu and Dale and Sydney and whoever else from the Boston tribe could get there, to find some place to be for the next phase of this revolution that I couldn't draw a picture of, after the trial and whatever that brought.

But when I talked to Sarah the night before my father and I left Urbana, she was riddled with doubts, asking me all these questions that I could tell were coming from her parents. I had hoped she would come to Illinois—a third of the way toward our California goal—until we got it together to head west. But she was adamantly against that, saying that she could make more money in Philly and that she didn't want to leave there until we had a clear idea of the next step. How would we get to California? Where would we stay? What would we do? Shit, it was like *she* wanted me to draw a picture of our future. She talked about some cousin who was running some kind of television studio in Los Angeles where maybe she could get a job. That wasn't the California I was dreaming of.

The ten days Sarah and I were together on the road trip, comrades and lovers traveling through a hostile land, brave and free, were so cool. Really together in a way we hadn't been in months. She was great talking to the cops in Oxford, getting Mike out of jail. She held her own in the bars and clubs in Champaign-Urbana. My friends dug her. My parents and sisters loved her. She rolled easily through a steady stream of friends and family and happenings and was just as eager and passionate as I was when we stole a few moments alone to make love on the sofa bed in my parents' basement. It was the best time we had had together. To me, it was a prelude to the bigger trip, the endless trip we would begin as soon as a few petty details were cleared up. But for her … I don't know.

My father and I had decided to make the trip to Boston because we were frustrated with the lack of communication from our lawyers and thought a face-to-face meeting might help. That was the justification, at least, but I knew both of us just needed to get away from Urbana for our own different reasons. We did well together on the road. He drove. I navigated, following the bold blue lines on the AAA Triptik. We focused on the task at hand. Where would we stop for lunch, for gas? Were we on track to make our overnight destination in time for our six o'clock dinner? We talked baseball—the Red Sox were in the midst of a losing streak, but the season was still young, so we could still hope—and the distant politics of Republicans and Democrats.

But when we got to the room at the motel, my father asked me if I minded if he had a drink from a vodka bottle he had brought along on our trip. What could I say? Then he had a couple of beers with dinner, and after we came back, while I was in the bathroom, when he didn't think I could hear him, he made a call to find out where the closest bar was. He told me he had to check something with the front desk. He disappeared for an hour or so and came back smelling of booze and mints, smiling like a little kid who just stole some candy and thought he got away with it. And tried to engage me in meaningful conversation.

"The system drills it into us that there are no possible alternatives to the way things are, so we give up," I said. I knew it was sort of pointless having this discussion with him in his condition, and it was a discussion we'd already had many times in various contexts, but it was just me and him in a motel in Erie, Pennsylvania, and I didn't have a whole lot else to do. "We stop trying. We accept our distorted roles in life and try to find ways to cope with that." I paused, giving him a steady look and smiling, but I don't think he picked up that it was aimed at him. "So, first we have to say 'no' to what is, to break away from the system's hold on us. Only then can we begin to understand and build an alternative reality."

"That's a cop-out, and you know it," he said, with a belligerent edge. But I wasn't taking his bait, as I had so many other times. It was just sad to me. Released from the pressures and inhibitions he faced at home, his first move was to get drunk and I was his implicit accomplice—just the boys on a road trip. But we weren't drinking together. Even though I drank freely with my friends it was never fun to drink with him—and I was still officially too young to drink. Now, he was putting some safe distance between us. Since my arrest, our talks had become realer, less confrontational. More and more, I think, he was starting to understand why I was a freak, and I understood why that was scary for him. A lot of what being a freak meant was a direct renunciation of much of his life. And he saw no way out. He kept wanting me to explain myself in terms that didn't mean a rejection of him. Abbie Hoffman told us we all have to kill our parents. He meant that figuratively, of course—kill the values and fear of authority represented by our parents. But now, in a frighteningly vivid way, I was watching my father die, his spirit at least, and it was me who was killing him. I couldn't feel too good about that, to claim some kind of victory. And it seemed like his challenging tone as he lay on the other bed at the Erie Holiday Inn, no doubt bolstered by the deceitful certainty of a few stiff drinks, was an opening salvo of a stand he was determined to make. But I wasn't in any mood to try to finish him off.

"Maybe it is a cop-out," I said. "I'm sorry I don't have a better answer for you, but I don't. I know I've got to try this way, to see where it leads. I hope someday I can explain it better, in a way that you can understand." I smiled. "I'll keep working on that picture."

He looked a little confused by my passivity, but claimed his own victory of sorts: "Well, I hope so, too." But his tone had softened.

"Hey, I'm tired," I said. "Bet you're tired, too. Maybe we should try to get some sleep. We've got plenty of miles in front of us tomorrow to solve the world's problems."

He agreed and got up and turned on the TV. A movie, *Dark at the Top of the Stairs*, had just started. We watched it in silence until soon I heard my father's deep snores. I wasn't really tired and I was also trying to write a letter to Sarah, which I started by quoting the entire lyrics to Sam Cooke's "A Change is Gonna Come" ("It's been a long time coming"). I got into the movie. A husband and wife argue until the husband storms out. The wife struggles with her adolescent kids and unsympathetic relatives. A troubled teenager, isolated and distant partly because of his over-ambitious mother and partly because he was a Jew in small-town Oklahoma, commits suicide, which freaks everybody out. Everybody's pretty fucked up but it was a good movie and somehow the family moves to some sort of reconciliation, not a happily-ever-after kind of thing but a believable sense of appreciation of each other, I guess. On the pad where I had started the letter to Sarah, I wrote down something that Cora, the wife and mother, said: "The people we love aren't always perfect, are they? But if we love them, we have to take them as they are."

The movie ended with the kids going out to the movies and the parents heading up the stairs, where I guess it wasn't quite so dark anymore, to make love. A hint of a tear formed in my eye.

The room echoed with my father's alcohol-amplified snoring. I felt guilty that I couldn't do anything but watch him drink himself to the courage he felt he needed to be with me alone, that I had complicated his already complicated life so much, and that all I wanted to do was get as far away as I could from him and his life. Wherever it was I was going, this trip to a place and a way of being that was mostly being shaped by negatives now— not the East, not the Midwest, not my parents, not Sarah's parents, not cities, not school, not jobs, not jail!—had no room for him. I had to drive. Could I navigate, too, with no bold blue lines to follow?

I turned the TV off and focused on writing to Sarah:

Sarah, sarah, sarah.

There's a lot on my mind and I'm not sure how it's gonna come out. I was doing fine when I was sure we were merely in a resting place in our great adventure and soon Philadelphia and Urbana would be far behind. But after talking to you last night it seems like we are back to where we were before we left Boston. I felt like over the ten days we were together that we had finally beaten back all the doubts and hang-ups that were keeping us from being together and getting things ready to head west. But after talking to you, I just don't know anymore …

June 15, 1970 [Philadelphia]

I had to wear a stupid fake white straw hat and a red-and-white striped barbershop quartet kind of shirt. But that wasn't even the worst part. One of the women I was staying with in downtown Philadelphia had told me about an art show in Rittenhouse Square where some of her friends were exhibiting and I suggested to my boss, who hadn't heard anything about it, that I take my hot-dog cart there. He did send one of the carts to that show, but not me. Instead, I was assigned to a Win the War in Vietnam rally at Washington Square Park, just around the corner from the Liberty Bell and all those famous patriotic sites. He even told me to tuck my hair up into my hat to look less threatening to the pro-war folks. Asshole.

I had come down to Philly a couple weeks before. I'd stayed behind in Boston after my father went back to Urbana. The meeting with the lawyers was strange. Orsini—who I only saw when my mother or father was in town; I usually just saw the assistant Zinzer—said the cops and prosecutors were still intent on going after me hard, to make an example of me for assaulting cops at a riot, and especially because one was a Black hero cop. Orsini's strategy was to try to keep postponing the trial as long as he could, hoping things would cool down. September was the soonest it would happen, which at least gave us the whole summer before we had to deal with it.

Orsini also told us that the shrink had called me a sociopath, or said that I had "strong sociopathic tendencies," basically the same thing. Even though we had all agreed that I should plead not guilty, rather than plead guilty and use my personality disorder as a reason for leniency, the shrink said I needed serious psychiatric treatment. My father was, of course, deeply concerned and wanted me to set up some appointments right away, but I hated that shrink and I really didn't have any interest in psychiatric treatment. It was the same old shit: resisting an insane society makes you insane.

I needed to get away from the paranoia I couldn't avoid in Boston. Get some place—with Sarah—where I could clear my head.

I couldn't go back to Illinois. I couldn't get Sarah to go there. I was staying with some friends in Boston and tried to talk Sarah into coming up there until we headed west—whenever that might be. That wasn't happening. So one of the guys I was staying with in Boston told me about a good friend with an apartment in downtown Philly who had an extra bed. So I hitchhiked down there, knowing that I had a much better chance of getting Sarah to leave if we were together. When we were together, we were together. She was a different person than she was at the other end of the telephone or a letter. She had faith in us. She was open to risk and adventure and not knowing. We talked things through. We were a couple. We were together. But when we were apart, she seemed overcome by guilt and doubt and reasons not to do anything. So I found a way to be in Philly without being in the suburbs and dependent on her parents.

Some friend of the folks I was staying with told me about the job with the hot-dog carts—and I needed money. It was kind of a goof, anyway, selling hot dogs on the street, something I could write about someday. At first, even the costume just seemed sort of funny. I was on a corner near City Hall the first two days, and I did all right. They were good hot dogs, especially with mustard and kraut. They wanted us to sell at least 200 a day and I got close, 175 or 180 both days. And I got ten cents a dog, so I made about thirty-five bucks those first two days and they seemed happy enough with me. Guess they figured I'd be up to my quota in no time.

But then they sent me to the stupid pro-war rally instead of the art show. I was pissed. First of all, it was a pitiful crowd. The number of pro-war people was dwindling rapidly as Nixon's Vietnamization strategy floundered like all previous policies, and people were still reeling from the reactions to the invasion of Cambodia and the Kent State killings. And war supporters were not the type to go to a rally on a perfectly fine June Sunday afternoon. The organizers of the rally made me set up on a corner opposite the park, so most of the few people who did show up didn't even see my cart. And, as I mentioned, I was pissed, so I didn't even try to show the upbeat customer attraction skills I'd worked on my first two days. One guy, all decked out in red, white, and blue asked me if he could put a "Win the War" sticker on my cart. No, man, you can't, I told him, with no pretense of being nice. Another part of the job was that I was supposed to give free hot dogs to any cop who came by. I did it because I think the owners were on some shaky ground with their permits and such. But I made up for that—in my own mind—by giving free dogs to any little Black kids that wandered by, counting those on my cop tally.

Sarah showed up in the middle of the afternoon as the rally was winding down. I saw her wandering around in the park across the street looking confused, looking for me. I saw her hair first, her mane of rolling rich brown curls moving among the crew cuts and bleached-out blonds, and then the soft pastels of her flowery shirt contrasted to the blunt blues and reds of the patriots—and then, when she saw me, her smile, a beacon amidst the sea of staggeringly straight people. And I could see her laugh as she crossed the street toward me. Man, it was good to see her.

"Interesting place to see you, Ben Tucker," she said and gave me a quick sweet kiss. "I looked for you at Rittenhouse Square and saw a hot-dog cart—but not you."

"Yeah, that was the owner's girlfriend. Can you believe they sent me here?" I didn't care if anybody heard me. I didn't care if I ever sold another hot dog.

"It's almost funny," she said, looking around as the crowd slowly dispersed across the way. She could see it still wasn't funny to me. "But it's a pisser they sent somebody else to the art show when it was your idea. I'm sorry, Ben."

"I can't do this anymore," I said. "I've sold maybe fifty hot dogs. I've been up since seven and out here for five hours—and I'm going to make five bucks. And to be surrounded by all these rah-rah America, silent majority assholes."

"I'm sorry," she said, but she couldn't help laughing. I glared at her. "C'mon, Ben, this is so absurd, you have to admit it." She came around to my side of the cart and gave me a big hug that knocked my hat off. I shook my head to loosen up my hair, ran my fingers through it to set it free, and looked into Sarah's eyes shining into me and her big wide smile.

I kinda laughed. "Yeah, you're right," I said. "Fuck 'em."

With Sarah's encouragement, I decided to pack it in and roll my cart the seven blocks back to the shop, instead of waiting for them to come pick me up. My boss was upset that I quit early and that I hadn't sold very many hot dogs. But before they could fire me, I quit, letting them know just how pissed I was. And then they told me I had to come back in a couple of days to get paid. Assholes to the end.

Sarah and I went to a funky little sandwich shop across the street from where I was staying. We ordered a large egg salad hoagie with lots of tomatoes and split it. It was great. She treated. Since I hadn't gotten paid for my hot dog sales, I had less money than when I got there.

The hot dog job had lifted my spirits. I'd come to Philadelphia, found work, tried to show patience, only gently coaxing Sarah to get her shit together so we could head west. I had taken initiative rather than waiting for things to happen. And I sensed some movement. But now I felt like I had gotten nowhere. I couldn't play this fucking game, pretending to be the kind of responsible person that would ease the fears of Sarah's parents or even maybe Sarah's own fears.

"This isn't working, Sarah. I don't know what I was trying to do," I said, wiping oozing egg salad from my chin. I was feeling beaten. "No that's not true. I do know what I was trying to do. I was trying to get you to leave. But I don't know why I thought it would work. Maybe I thought I had as much power over you as your parents think I do. But I can't do this and I don't feel any closer to getting out of here than I did when I got here."

"I know why you came, maybe I needed you to come, to whisk me away to foreign lands," Sarah said, with a little twinkle and a watery warmth in her soft brown eyes. "I'm glad you came. My parents are driving me crazy, treating me like a kid. We go see the shrink, which they insisted I do—and she tells them they have to let me live my life, but they don't seem to hear that part. My brother lectures me, says that I'm breaking up the family. I don't know where my head would be if you weren't here to remind me that I do have a life of my own. I want to be whisked away from all this. I'm just not ready to leave yet, but I'm getting there. Really."

I let out a deep sigh. How beaten could I be? Sarah was right there, looking so good, glowing with unmistakable love, sharing this delicious sandwich with me and not saying no, just asking for a little more patience. Man, she made it hard to be as demanding as I wanted to be.

"Yeah, okay." I said drawing another long breath. "We just don't have unlimited time. It's been a month since the road trip and we have maybe two and a half months until we have to be back for the trial—and California is a long way away."

"I need maybe two more weeks," she said. She studied me, reading my reaction. Two weeks seemed like a long time but this was the first time she had offered a somewhat firm departure time, so I forced a little smile. "I am really glad you came," she said, "and watching you try to make it work—selling hot dogs—you did look very cute in your uniform—sleeping on a tiny cot, trying to fit my schedule … It did work, Ben. I want to be with you. I want to travel with you. Just please give me this time. I can make some more money. Maybe I can even soften my parents. It'll be better. Really."

Sometimes losing ends up looking a lot like winning. What could I say? I couldn't ask any more than that from her. I reached out and grabbed her hand across the table. We just kind of stared into each other's eyes for a while.

"Yeah, sure." I said. "I love you."

"I love you, too," she said.

"I think I should go back to Boston, though. I don't have a job anymore. It's a little weird where I'm staying and it seems like it just makes it harder on you. It's not like it's that easy for us to get together." Sarah was working almost full time at Saks Fifth Avenue on the Mainline. I visited her a couple of times. I loved the way she looked in the dress-up kind of clothes she had to wear. It was like she was in a disguise and only I knew what a total freak was lurking inside those dresses and fancy skirts and blouses and all that really turned me on. But it was always awkward when I went there. And I sort of blew her cover—no question that I was a freak—though she didn't seem to really care. But the store was a long way from where I was staying and her parents' house was even farther, way out in the suburbs, so my being in Philly did greatly complicate her life. "Maybe it will be easier for you to wrap things up here if I'm not around."

She started to protest, but then acknowledged that was true.

"I can deal with two more weeks apart if it means getting closer to a whole summer together," I said. "You do what you've got to do here, and I'll go to Boston and try to find us a ride west. You come up as soon as you can."

She smiled and squeezed my hand. She cleaned off our table and threw away the trash. I put my arm around her shoulder and she put hers around my waist and we pulled close together and walked slowly down the busy street.

July 6, 1970 [El Paso, Texas]

Will Poore seemed a little scattered as he left us in the motel, heading out to cross the Rio Grande to Juarez to get a divorce. Sarah and I were anxious in a different kind of way. As soon as we heard his VW puttering out of the parking lot, we stretched out on the double bed in the cheap room. Big smiles.

"Maybe we should take a shower first," Sarah said.

"I don't need no stinking shower," I said and pulled her close into me and we kissed a long deep kiss, a long deferred kiss, hard and demanding at first, but slowly easing into a smooth melding of yielding lips. She tasted so good. We'd been on the road for almost four days, long hours in the car and spent the night before sleeping on the ground in a rest area (after one night in the good old rollaway in my parents' basement in Urbana), and now we were alone in a real bed. We'd been so close in the tight spaces of Will's little bug or curled up in sleeping bags, rubbing up against each other, breathing in each other's ripening scent, touching and laughing and catching long and longing glances of each other as the states rolled by. Now, with Will off to do the deed that was the reason we were going from Boston to San Francisco via El Paso, we were free to shed our clothes and make steaming love while the noisy air conditioner shielded us from the crazy heat outside.

Richly satisfied, we just lay there, quiet for a while. We had just made love in fucking El Paso, Texas. What a trip. We were indeed in foreign territory. Texas!

I had seen Will's notice seeking riders for his strange cross-country route in the BU Union. We talked. I liked him. He seemed to like me. I think he liked the fact that we were a couple. I had to lie a little bit about being able to drive a stick shift—he wanted us to share driving—and Sarah could for sure. But I had messed around with Sarah's bug and Barry had one of those automatic-stick shift VWs that were kinda like driving a stick. I was sure I could fake it until I learned.

Sarah had come up to Boston so we could leave from there without a detour to Philly. We had saved a little bit of money, Sarah more than me, of course, but we had both gone back to the Philly hot dog company to collect all $76 of the pay they owed me before I headed back to Boston. They had tried to stiff me out of most of it, saying I had cost them money by quitting all of a sudden. I probably would have just told them to get fucked and split, but Sarah was tenacious and they finally gave me all of it. So, we had a decent stake for our trip and when we got things lined up with Will, our westward pilgrimage became a reality.

Things got a little complicated because I lost my wallet the night before we left. It didn't have any of our money— fortunately Sarah was keeping all that—but it did have a Texaco credit card (they would give them to *anybody*) and my drivers' license and I was committed to sharing the driving. With all the legal problems I was already entangled in, driving across the country with no ID was a little risky. But nothing was going to stop or delay this trip for me.

It didn't take long for Will to realize that I couldn't really drive a stick. But he was a nice guy and was patient with me and would help me get through the gears, me working the clutch, him the gear shift, until we got on the highway, where I could just cruise. I was a great driver and good for long distances once I got past the shifting part. He appreciated that.

After our overnight stay in Urbana, we headed toward Tulsa, Oklahoma. It was the 4th of July. As darkness slowly crept over the high plateau of southwestern Missouri, we were treated to a series of fireworks displays, off in the distance, on either side of the interstate. We had ventured beyond our known world and off into this wide wide world called the USA. In each of those little towns with colors exploding over them, kids were oohing and ahhing, balconies were decked out in red, white, and blue, and bad local bands were jerking pride out of deeply loyal Americans with tinny versions of "Stars and Stripes Forever." I didn't know exactly where Merle Haggard's Muskogee was but I sensed it wasn't too far away. It was cool seeing the night sky unexpectedly brighten with fireworks, but I didn't think we would be welcome in any of those little towns, who were celebrating something we were no longer a part of. It was an odd sensation rolling down Interstate 44, feeling a surge of a Woody Guthrie kind of patriotism at the immensity and openness and variety of my country—it was still my country—while feeling no joy or pride at what my country had become, what those people in Fidelity or Loma Linda or Afton said they loved so righteously. "Love it or leave it," they told us. And that's just what we were trying to do, leaving to make something new to love, "somewhere where we might laugh again … very free and easy … We are leaving. They don't need us."

At the rest stop outside Tulsa that night, we slept under an immense Oklahoma sky, a fireworks show of a different sort, more stars, brighter than I had ever seen, even in the wide horizons of the Illinois farm country. Curling up next to Sarah in our sleeping bags, I was humbled and inspired by that sky in a way all the little dots of small-town fireworks could never do. It shined for all of us, for freaks and Blacks and the Vietnamese, for the Indians who had been driven here in tears and the enslaved Africans they brought with them, for the dust bowl emigrants and the small-time farmers trying to eke out a living from these tired soils and hard seasons, for the kids fighting our war and the kids dying under our bombs, for "every hung-up person in the whole wide universe"—and, yeah, even for the straight White assholes who thought God had picked them and this arrangement of privilege called the United States of America to reap the riches of the earth and to lord them over all other peoples. That sky was a blazing testament that we're all in this together and that understanding that truth and living by it was the only sane way to get out of the mess we had made of the world. Yet, to the good ole folks of heartland America, it was us who were crazy.

From Tulsa, we put in a long day and night driving across Oklahoma and Texas. I did a six-hour stint behind the wheel through West Texas, passing by Bug Spring and Midland and Odessa. We had decided to push to get as close to El Paso as we could, driving through the night when the temperatures had cooled down a bit, so Will could get an early start on his Mexican divorce and Sarah and I could hide out in a cheap air-conditioned motel through the heat of the day. For some reason, Pecos, which we rolled by about midnight, particularly scared me. Maybe because of an old memory of some bad Western fueled by the crazy hallucinatory thoughts that rush through your brain after days and days and hours and hours of staring at the white lines—to the point where you can see them going away from you rather than vanishing beneath your wheels—I became convinced that a roadblock of Texas Rangers was waiting just up ahead, ready to toss me in a cell I couldn't get out of—all because I'd lost my stupid drivers' license.

But we sailed past Pecos, with no sign of any Rangers, and found a campground at about three in the morning on a scraggly dusty brown mountainside twenty miles outside of El Paso, to try to sleep for a few hours before finding a motel.

Now in the dark cool of the motel room, Sarah and I lay in the bed for a while, reveling in the aftermath of love and the softness of the mattress. But we started getting hungry, so we roused ourselves to take a shower. It was a small shower but we managed to both get in there. She had her back to the shower head, facing me, with my back against the shower wall. I loved watching the water run down through her thick hair, flow over her shoulders, and cascade over her magnificent breasts, like a mountain stream over sudden majestic boulders. We couldn't avoid rubbing up against each other, and we kissed, a soft very wet kiss, but we tried to stick to the business of soaping each other up and washing away the grime of the road.

We dressed and headed outside to look for something to eat. We were blasted back by the heat of the noontime sun as soon as we opened the door. Holding our hands up against the glare as if to shield ourselves, we started across the parking lot, but didn't get far before the hot black asphalt burned against our soft bare feet. We scurried back, laughing at our foolishness. We put on some shoes and eventually survived the 100-foot trek to a great place that sold "burritos," a Mexican sort of food with meat and cheese and other stuff rolled up in a tortilla. They were great!

The air conditioning felt even better when we got back to the motel room. We eased into another, mellower lovemaking session and then Sarah fell asleep and I read from a couple of newspapers I'd picked up in the restaurant. The world was still churning away outside the bubble of our quest for love and land. The US Senate had "overwhelmingly" repealed the Gulf of Tonkin Resolution, the legislation based on lies that had been the initial justification for the fateful escalation of the

Vietnam War. Motherfuckers. Did that repeal somehow un-kill the 50,000 dead American soldiers and millions of Vietnamese soldiers and civilians? Race riots were raging in Asbury Park, a resort at the New Jersey shore. Nobody was quite sure what had triggered the riots, maybe just Black people getting fed up with serving the White folks who had the time and money to enjoy summer at their beautiful beaches. The Red Sox had beaten the Indians 8–4, led by big games from Petrocelli, Scott, and Conigliaro to go four games over .500, their high mark of the season so far.

Sports with their ups-and-downs and the occasional unbelievable upset could serve as a good diversion from the grim reality of war and racism that still hovered over all of us —wherever we went. But just as sports was spectacle, so was all this heavy shit in the papers, distant phenomena to cheer or frighten or anger us. The revolution, our revolution, was riding with us. We had won the battle for public opinion about the Vietnam War. Tricky Dick had named delegates to the sham peace talks in Paris while the bombing and the killing continued. But we couldn't fight the battles of the Black inner cities and had still not figured out how us White kids could effectively support Black revolutionaries. Sure, our westward pilgrimage was a getaway from the multilayers of constraints that the Old Country imposed on us but it was also a quest for a place we could make a stand, become the cultural, political, spiritual revolutionaries that we aspired to be. The revolution had to be us or it was just another phony entertainment for us spoiled kids of the American empire.

I drifted off to sleep, too, and Sarah and I napped off-and-on, cool and satisfied, until Will returned late in the afternoon, divorce papers in hand, ready for the final 1,200 miles to San Francisco.

July 16, 1970 [San Francisco]

Dear Family,

Greetings. We arrived safe and sound about a week ago. The trip was long and we were really glad to get out of that car. Texas was horrible—hot and dry and very long. We stayed in El Paso for a day and drove through the desert in New Mexico and Arizona during the night. I was driving at dawn in Arizona. Sarah and Will were sleeping. It was really beautiful, a clear pink light illuminating tall stately cactus, spread out across the desert with little clumps of mountains in the background. I still can't quite believe we are in San Francisco, a city we've heard about and dreamed about for so long. It really is a cool city. People in general are friendlier than any other place I've ever been. We've been staying with Mitch—one of the guys who lived here moved out so we are renting that room for the rest of the month. Jobs are very tight here. I was pretty sure I could get a job at the leather place where Mitch works. The guy who runs it is a friend from the band days, but there's been a lot of friction there lately and he doesn't wanna hire any more friends at least until Aug. 1. By that time, Herschel and Mike and other people from Boston should be here with vans so we will probably go camping around California and Oregon and Colorado.

*So far we've just been getting into the city—getting adjusted to being in ****CALIFORNIA**** and figuring out where we're going to stay. Spent a lot of time in Berkeley. Very strange. Freaks everywhere and almost constant activity. Today Sarah and me ran into about six different people that we knew from Boston and Philly. Yesterday, hitching back from there, this guy picked us up and asked where we were from. After I said Illinois and Boston, he said he was staying with people from New Bedford. It turned out to be kids from* the Steele family, who we used to hang out with around the yacht club. He took us there but it was sort of awkward. We didn't have a lot to talk about.

We've been having a real good time. We're really here, two time zones further west than we've ever been. Everything seems new—and unreal. Today, I think we're going to Marin County which is across the Golden Gate Bridge and is s'pose to be very beautiful. There is s'pose to be a rock and roll festival there and some guy who picked us up hitchhiking gave us a free pass.

Oh—a bad note—I lost my wallet. It's been a long time since I've done that. I had a Texaco credit card in it. So could you send me any identification (birth certificate or something) that you might have and find out how I can get a duplicate driver's license—and draft card.

Well, I'm gonna sign off—hope everything goes well, with you, particularly, Dad, with your new job in Kankakee.

Love,

Ben

Dear Dr. & Mrs. Tucker, & Katherine & Cary (if you're there),

HI—we're having a really great time. Hope to see you all soon.

Love,

Sarah

August 6, 1970 [Half Moon Bay, California]

The tribe gathered on a beach at Half Moon Bay, the California of our dreams, a long soft tan sand beach, hugged by steep bluffs striped in shades of gold with curling white surf roaring out of the infinite blue sea. We had left Berkeley late in the morning, eight of us with two vehicles, an orange-striped VW bus and a deep green Ford van. Somehow the crazy plans we had sketched out, stoned and dreaming, on one edge of the continent, had worked and there we stood, after strange and tangled journeys, hovering over the other edge, speechless and smiling at all that lay before us.

Sarah and I had connected first with Dale and Sydney. They arrived in San Francisco in their VW bus about a week earlier, after an All-American scenic tour across the United States, stopping at Mount Rushmore and Yellowstone and places like that, taking their time, checking stuff out, kind of goofing on the tourist sites but digging them at the same time. They said some of that shit really is impressive.

Things had gotten strained for us at Mitch's. Mitch was still cool with us, but he was dealing with a complicated situation with his one-year-old son, and somebody else was anxious to move into our room. So we made it easier for him by splitting with Dale and Sydney for a trip to Yosemite. Man, what a spectacular place that was. We stayed at a campground called Tamarack Flat in the woods at an elevation of about 6,000 feet. The air was crazy clean and tall-tree fresh and light. I just wanted to drink it in until I burst. Sarah and I set up a sleeping place in a cool little nook between two big rocks and Dale and Sydney slept in their bus. It was the first time I've ever done any kind of real camping. I liked the basic feel of it. Your whole lives are just centered around eating and sleeping and wandering around in beautiful nature.

One night after we'd said good night and curled up in our sleeping bags, I remembered I'd left an almost empty bean can on the grate above the fire pit, something they explicitly told you not to do with all the critters lurking about. I went out to get it and just as I was leaning in to grab it, I saw another "hand" reaching toward it. I look up to see a bear about my height but with a few more pounds staring back at me. After a split second of a freaked-out stare down, we both turned and ran in opposite directions, me toward the shelter of the bus—yelling to Sarah to join me—and him back into the woods. I and then Sarah dove onto Dale and Sydney after they slid open the door for us. Once safe, the tangled mess of us broke out in survivors' laughter. Sarah and I hung there for a while until we cautiously returned to our nook, armed with pots and pans to rattle away any more unexpected night visitors. We weren't in the city anymore.

Dale and Sydney were kind of the grown-ups of our group. They had become a couple while a bunch of us—Sarah, Mike, Stu, Jeffrey, Patrick, Walter, and me—were all in the same dorm complex at Boston University. The summer after freshman year, they got an apartment up Commonwealth Avenue—1387—that became a central gathering point for the next year. Mike lived there that summer, then Jeffrey and Walter moved in when Mike and Stu and I moved to Mountfort Street, with Brian at that point. 1387 and Mountfort Street bracketed the BU campus and were the borders of our neighborhood as school faded in importance for all of us and drugs and rock and roll and revolution became the core of our curriculum. But 1387 wasn't just 30 blocks away from Mountfort Street, it was an entirely different scene: neat, regular meals, an order to how they dealt with guests and visitors, never the crash pad atmosphere of Mountfort Street. They would send kids looking for a place to sleep to us with our "Welcome All" greeting on our front door. Maybe it was entirely the influence of Sydney, a woman's touch. We never had a woman living at Mountfort Street, despite my yearlong effort to persuade Sarah. But it was more than just the woman thing, I think. It was them as a couple. They were solid, steady, had a plan, like their itinerary for their cross-country trip and even the trip to Yosemite. They always seemed to know what they were doing, where they were going.

Dale was a little under six-feet tall, built lean and sturdy, had thin blond hair that always seemed to stop just short of his collar and a wispy light mustache. Raised in Richmond, Virginia, he played guitar and had a trace of a southern accent that he would exaggerate when he popped off a little riff of folk wisdom: "What other people think don't leave a blue mark" and such. Sydney was pretty and knew it. She had a smooth oval face and a worldly smile. She was skinny in an attractive way and had long straight dark hair that hung down well past her shoulders. Her beloved cat Snookly had been the prince of 1387 and a pampered passenger on their cross-country trek.

We got back to the Bay Area just about the time Stu was arriving on a bus from Salt Lake City. A big old house in Berkeley with a Mountfort Street feel to it—funky and chaotic and welcoming, but with a functioning telephone—served as our West Coast message board and meeting place. A guy named Steve who we all knew from BU days lived there. That's where Dale and Sydney and Sarah and I met up with Stu, who beamed at the sight of us and then shifted immediately to mock anger, "Where the fuck you guys been? I travel all the way across country to see you and you're off vacationing somewhere."

"Stuey, my brother," Dale said. "We've just been biding our time until you got here, so the real fun can begin." He lit up a joint and passed it to Stu.

"That's better," Stu said before taking a deep toke and handing the joint to me. Stu was a little taller than me and a little shorter than Dale and his thick black hair flared out almost to his shoulders. In between hits, he regaled us with the tale of his trip, rolling on the hard edges and soft r's of his Worcester, Massachusetts, accent.

He started out with friends of our friends from the Bronx—the "boys from New York," we called them—Really Big Mike and Berkovich. They were planning to drive all the way to the West Coast. "But man, they started getting on my nerves right away. They were like two old yentas, just bitching and hassling each other," he said, reliving his exasperation. "It was crazy, man, these two freaks acting like two irritable old ladies. And then, they stopped at some farm in Indiana where some friends lived, and that was cool for a couple days—at least it was a break from them constantly kvetching at each other—and that's exactly what it was." He paused to take another toke, sucking it in deep. The other four of us, well on our way to being stoned, looked at each other, chuckling, glad that Stu was now there with us.

He let out the smoke and saw us all smiling at him "But for some reason, I wanted to get out here to find you guys. We got back in the car and it was the same old shit, but at least we were making progress west. Then ... " his annoyance flaring like he was back in that car all over again." ... we cross the Mississippi into St. Louis and they start talking about going to visit some farm in Missouri, and I said, 'That's it. Let me out. Right here! Right now!' So I got out right in front of the arch and started hitchhiking."

Stu got a ride pretty quickly, and, he said, the guy was so impressed that he was hitchhiking all the way across the country to meet up with some friends—he said, "They must be really good friends"—that he gave him a ride all the way to Glenwood Springs, Colorado. But when Stu tried to hitchhike there, a cop pulled him over and told him. "Hitchhiking is illegal in Colorado, so you've got two choices: I can give you a ride to jail or I can give you a ride to the bus station in town." Soon, he was on a bus to Salt Lake City. Having grown up in the grimy, postindustrial melting pot Northeast, Stu walked around that Mormon city in amazement: "Holy shit, man. It was the cleanest city I ever saw and nothing but White people. I kept thinking, 'What is this city? Where am I?'" He thought about hitchhiking the rest of the way, but he had enough money for another bus and the urge to get to California as soon as he could won out.

So … we were five.

That night Stu, Sarah, and I slept on couches at Steve's place and Dale and Sydney slept in their bus. About the time we were all groping for coffee the next morning, the phone rang and it was Mike (only sorta big Mike, our Mountfort Street roommate). He and Herschel and Rusty were somewhere nearby in Berkeley, having driven all night in their final push on their journey from Champaign. Somebody gave them directions, and soon the eight of us awkwardly filled the living room of the big house, as the people who actually lived there made their way around us, trying to be cool but unmistakably and understandably uncomfortable with our sudden takeover.

But, shit. man. We were all in fucking California!

Mike had stayed in Champaign since our late spring road trip from Boston to Kansas City. He fell right in with my old friends, living with Scotty and Alexander at 501, hanging out with the

band—no longer the Seeds of Doubt, now called Mud—making
the bar circuit, partying and drinking and scrounging meals and
dope from wherever he could. He loved it. He wasn't ready to
leave when Sarah and I had stopped there with Will Poore on
our trip west. But Herschel—a grad student at BU who had
moved into Mountfort Street for our last couple of months after
Brian had moved out and was sometimes my partner in writing
papers for hire—had bought a van and met up with Larry in
Champaign. Rusty had come back to Champaign from a tour
with the Navy in Vietnam, ready to party all that shit out of his
head. At a bar one night, when Herschel and Mike were talking
about setting out for California and this great adventure with
some freaks from Boston, he thought that sounded like fun and
decided to come along.

Somebody lit a joint and Steve and a couple of his
roommates squeezed in to take some tokes. Mike and Herschel
and Rusty were fried, still feeling the road underneath them, but
we were all giddy from the rush of being together and ready to
get out of that jammed crash pad, out of the city and its sirens
and congestion, ready to get on with whatever it was we had
all come this long way to do. Head west toward the water, we
decided, and south toward open beaches.

It was late afternoon when we pulled into a parking lot in
Half Moon Bay. It was a perfect day, rich blue sky, soft wind off
the water cooling the air to a pleasant warmth, just short of hot.
We piled out of the van and the bus, slowly, all of us stretching,
not in any kind of unison but with a certain common sense of
purpose, toward the western sun, shining—it seemed in that
moment—just for us. How far this was from my last lonely walk
in Boston, slipping through the siege of the TPF, hunched into
my coat, my hair hidden in my hat. Standing on that bluff over

that beach, the gentle warm breeze teased through my hair like a lover's fingers, sending tingly shivers all over—shivers of love and unknown freedom and an unbounded ocean of possibility.

I found Sarah's eyes and reached for her. We hugged. We'd won something. This was really something. Then Stu and Mike and Dale and Sydney and Herschel and Rusty. Hugs and backslaps all around. We were on our way.

August 11–12 [Mendocino]

Sydney made a supper of hamburger, onions, and potatoes, cooked over the fire, and a salad of cucumber, tomato, and lettuce. It was real good. Sydney was amazing in how she could put together cheap, simple food and make it taste so good. We were camping in Mendocino on one more spectacular California beach. Our camp was backed up against the curl of a steep cliff. A lot of other people were camping on the beach, too, some of them in crude but creative shelters crafted out of driftwood. After supper, some cat came by and shared some wine with us. Soon after that, another guy turned us on to some dope and had some psilocybin for sale. Herschel was the only one into it and he dropped it right away. Other people kept wandering over and hanging out by the fire. It was a mellow scene, the fire crackling, smoke drifting around, getting in one person's face for a while, then shifting to somebody else. The easy buzz of the wine lifted up by the pot was perfect, as the conversation wafted around in soft tones beneath the roar of the waves just a few dozen yards away.

Amazingly, one of the people who drifted into our camp was a kid name Mark, who I knew from Boston. We weren't all that tight but we kept running into each other in odd places—demonstrations, sub shops, a beach in California 3,000 miles from our last meeting place. It was cool to see him here, and we were just getting over our amazement at the way our paths kept crossing when this old—forty or so—wino in a nearby driftwood hut started yelling enraged profanities at a girl who had apparently suggested he stop drinking: "Who the fuck are you to tell me what to do, bitch?" The easy talk and laughter around our campfire stopped and Rusty and Mike, who were sitting closest to the wino's hut stood up to see what was going on. The girl yelled something back at him and split down the beach and things got quiet for a bit and we got back to our good times, Dale playing some soft guitar and quiet conversations going around. But then the girl, who had come back, said something to the wino, who started screaming again and grabbed her and threw her toward their fire. She rolled off the edge of the firepit—and came running over to our camp, where we all surrounded her, Sydney and Sarah especially checking her out to make sure she was okay.

She—her name was Vicky—was kind of drunk herself. Three other people who'd been partying with them followed her to our camp, too, abandoning the wino—Billy was his name— who continued to rant, now in our direction. We tried to ignore him hoping he'd pass out and shut up. Then he started talking shit about Jews. "Can't go anywhere in this fucking country without being surrounded by fucking kikes. Fucking ruining everything." I don't know if this was his standard rap or, if he, in his stupor, somehow detected the Jews among us—Sarah, Stu, Mike, and Herschel. I could see Mike fuming and this was all totally freaking out Herschel, who by now was flying on that psilocybin and kind of huddled behind us, up against the cliff wall.

"Hey, man, why don't you shut up and leave us alone," Rusty finally yelled back at him. "Nobody wants to listen to your hateful bullshit."

"Yeah, yeah," Billy yelled back. "Fucking kikes can't take a joke. Did you ever see a Jew laugh?"

"Nothing you're saying is funny," I said. "We were doing lots of laughing until you started bumming everybody out. Why don't you curl up with your jug and leave us alone."

"Fuck you," he yelled. "You don't look like a Jew to me, but you're worse because you kiss their ass." He took a big swill from his wine bottle. "Hey, you guys got a cigarette? The least you can do is give me a fucking cigarette."

We might have laughed if he didn't seem dangerous as well as being a fucking idiot. We went back to ignoring him again. He kept shouting for a cigarette but finally sunk back into his hut, and a little while later we saw him leave, carrying a passed-out friend over his shoulder.

Sydney and Dale split to sleep in their bus in the parking lot above the beach, and the rest of us, about ten altogether, including my Boston friend Mark and Vicky, gathered our sleeping bags in a tight circle for security, just in case Billy came back for Vicky or to strike out against his enemies, the Jews.

We had arrived in Mendocino on the sixth day of our collective quest. We had spent two nights at Half Moon Bay, mellowing out a bit after our various cross-country adventures, getting our bearings, figuring out some kind of plan. We needed to find a place to live. Sydney, Dale, Stu, and Herschel were ready to settle in right away—no obligations left on the East Coast.

My trial loomed and Sarah was still talking about going back to school at Temple. Mike was a key witness in my trial. Rusty was just going with the flow. But we wanted to find a place we could all come back to, a house big enough for us all, to serve as a base. From there, we could look for land to establish a farming commune where we could survive outside of the system, learn self-defense to protect ourselves from the pigs, and see what wondrous things we could do with our creative energy set free: books and music and crafts and who knows what else. We didn't have a lot of money to secure a place—about $150 between us. We decided quickly that we weren't going to find anything we could afford heading south, that north of San Francisco was our best bet.

We had heard about an upcoming benefit concert for kids arrested in a riot in Palo Alto, just over the Santa Cruz Mountains from Half Moon Bay—four bands headed by Quicksilver. Sounded too good to miss. We'd hang out long enough to go to the concert then go back to Berkeley to see if we could find any leads on places and then head north.

The concert was in a bowl-like amphitheater that was great for hearing music but incredibly fucking hot. As soon as we got in, we decided we needed some cold beer to make it through, so Rusty and I worked our way back out through the crowd and found a nearby store to buy a case. That beer disappeared in a hurry. Even Sarah, who hated beer—I never saw her drink beer before—chugged one down. The show was great. The crowd was outasight—lots of dope working its way around. OooooOoOoOooo, have another hit!

This time, Berkeley struck me as depressing. Most of us crammed into Steve's place again, but Dale and Sydney took off to visit some relatives in nearby Belmont. I called home and talked to my mother. She sounded sad. I don't know why. My father had a new job working at an emergency room in Kankakee, almost 100 miles away from Urbana, but I don't know if that was it. Sometimes she just sounded disgusted and sick of life, made me feel bad to talk about our great expedition.

They couldn't do anything about my drivers' license. I had to be there to do that. And she had wired me money from my old band which was still slowly paying me off for what I'd put in for equipment, but she didn't know when I would get it. So we spent the whole next day waiting for Dale and Sydney to come back and checking Western Union for the money. I got real bummed out, started losing faith in the whole adventure. The transient nature of Berkeley—everybody we ran into was coming from somewhere else, looking for some new place, just like us—got to me. And just waiting for money to come from my parents, even though it was my money.

Sarah talked me through it. We had made it to California. We had met up with our friends. We'd be just fine even if the money didn't come. It wasn't worth getting all fucked up about. She was, of course, right and, once again, surprising. When we were struggling to get out of the East, she seemed so hesitant, so full of doubts. But now she was the source of strength and optimism. Man, I loved that girl.

The money never came but Dale and Sydney showed up about five o'clock and we headed north again, the eight of us plus a kid named Ras, who Mike knew from Boston, who was heading to Eugene, Oregon, which sounded like a pretty cool place.

We made it about eighty miles to a state beach just above Jenner, where there was a whole little community of people living in driftwood structures. We set up camp there. Sydney cooked up some delicious baked beans with onions and bacon and we discussed whether to head directly to Orleans, where Sydney's Uncle Lanny was supposedly living on a commune on forty acres of land or slowly working our way up the coast looking for a house. We decided on the second of those two options and Dale and Sydney announced they would kick in $60 for our house fund, making it just about $200.

Mendocino was our next stop.

We survived our first night in Mendocino with no further hassles from Billy. The next morning, after a cup of hobo coffee on the beach, we walked up the bluff and into town and the Pyewacket Cafe, a far-out little place, where a twenty-cent cup of coffee buys you a place to sit as long as you wanted. They also had these great muffins with raisins and nuts for a dime! We hung out there for a long time, talking to local freaks about possible places to rent. They always kind of rolled their eyes when we told them what we were looking for, a place for eight people, maybe more, and what we could pay for rent: $50 to $75 a month. But they were cool. One guy knew Walter from Boston and asked if we were part of the great caravan heading west. Yes, I guess we were.

I also got caught up with some old newspapers that were piled up by the dirty dish bins at the Pyewacket. Crazy shit in Marin County. Black revolutionaries had smuggled weapons into the county courthouse during the trial of a prisoner accused of stabbing a White guard, kidnapped the judge and other hostages, and fought a gun battle with police as they were trying to get away. The judge and three of the four revolutionaries were killed, including Jonathan Jackson, the seventeen-year-old brother of George Jackson, one of the Soledad Brothers, who had been accused of killing a prison guard at Soledad Prison.

The death of that guard came three days after three Black inmates had been killed by a sharpshooter at that prison. The case of the Soledad Brothers had garnered widespread attention among activists, led by well-known Communist activist Angela Davis, a professor of philosophy at UCLA. The courthouse revolutionaries had demanded immediate release of the Soledad Brothers. The papers said that Davis had bought the weapons that young Jackson had smuggled into the courthouse and that she was now on the run, a fugitive. Wow. That courthouse was just a few hours south of Mendocino, but we were worlds away from the shit that went down there.

With no leads on a house to follow up on after we left the Pyewacket, we spent the rest the day on the beach, collecting incredibly beautiful abalone shells and playing cribbage. Rusty had taught us to play—the only good thing to come out of his Navy experience, he said—and the cool jargon that goes along with it: "his nobs" and "his nibs" and "hauling timber," which meant to cheat, pegging more spots than you were entitled to. We had a good time, though Rusty and Herschel beat Sarah and me, five games to four.

Beyond his cribbage exploits, Rusty didn't talk much about the war or his time in the service. His straight black hair, matched by a thick black mustache, was starting to get a little length to it, sweeping across his forehead, like an early Beatles cut. He didn't talk a lot about anything. He was sort of an outsider to the other seven of us who'd gone through so much together in Boston. But he was a mellow, solid guy, did his share of gathering firewood or whatever else needed to be done. He didn't seem real concerned about where we were going or what we were going to do, just digging hanging out with us, living on beaches, at the other end of the Pacific Ocean from the ship he'd been stationed on.

After the cribbage match, Mark—the guy I kept seeing in strange places—suddenly got stone serious and told me he thought the cosmic reason he had run into me on this California beach was to tell me not to go back east, that only bad things would happen to me there, that I should find a place to hole up in the West and create a new life, leave that all behind. I could tell his concern was coming from his heart and it did give me something to think about. Sarah and Mike and Rusty all joined in the conversation.

"We definitely could protect you," Mike said. "You know those assholes are out to fuck you in court. Man, you really should think about disappearing."

"But what kind of life could we have?" Sarah said. "We couldn't have any contact with any friends or family."

"Always be looking over your shoulder," Rusty said.

"There's ways around that," Mike said. "Better fucking life than if Tucker's in jail."

"But Mike, even you, even everybody here—we couldn't see any of you. Unless you wanted to disappear with us," Sarah said. I liked that she assumed it was an "us" that would disappear, but she was right, we'd have to be cut off from everybody. "Would you do that, Mike?"

"Shit, yeah, you know I would," Mike said. "I got nothing to go back to."

"Jail could fuck you up forever," Mark said to me. He had a ragged beard and a necklace made from glistening shells he had found that morning. "Man, I know that's why I'm here. Don't go back, I'm telling you."

"I don't know," I said. "Thanks, I know you all are thinking about what's best for me. But I don't know. The cops are lying so I think I have about a fifty-fifty chance of getting off. And even if I'm convicted, I think maybe I have a fifty percent chance of not going to prison. And it's almost certain that I would appeal if I was found guilty, that would give me enough time to get out of the country or go underground. I just don't know that I could live with the paranoia of being on the run unless I don't have any other choices."

Mark shook his head. "So, you're willing to accept—even if all your odds are right—a one in four in chance of going to prison. Shit, man, I wouldn't do that. Who knows what will happen to you in there." He was absolutely sure of what I needed to do. Though I knew that there was no way to compare even the worst scenarios that could happen to me with what was happening to George Jackson, I couldn't help thinking about him as Mark's last words echoed through my head: Who knows what will happen?

Everybody got quiet, the wind suddenly whistling loudly above the crash of the waves.

Sarah gave me a look and we both got up and walked away from the camp, sat on a big flat rock at the end of the beach.

"It's a bummer he reminded us that the world is still going on, outside this beach," I said, "and unless we follow his advice and disappear, it's not long until we have to go back to it."

"Could you do that ... disappear?" she said as though she knew the answer.

"I don't know. You know, Sarah. I'm guilty. I hit one of those cops. We've been telling the story ... I don't know what happened to the rock I threw ... so long and so adamantly that sometimes I start to believe it's true. But just between you and me and the great big blue ocean, I just have to say it out loud. I'm fucking guilty. In some ways, it doesn't matter what the truth is, the pigs are going to say what they say and we'll say what we need to say … but you and me, we need to remember the truth."

She stared down at the rock for a while and finally said, "OK. Fine. You're guilty, but I can't disappear," she said, matter of fact, looking straight into my eyes. "You understand that. Right? I can't just blow off my family and all the rest of my life. I don't think you could either."

"Yeah," I said. There was something appealing about Mark's solution. Disappear. Let all that lawyer and court and freaked-out family stuff blow away, just toss it up into the stiff west wind and wave good-bye. Don't look back. I was more tempted by that path than Sarah, but she was right, I couldn't do it either. "So … what are we going to do?"

"I don't know. I don't think I really want to go back to school. I want to be with you somewhere … but I don't know."

Neither of us said anything for a while. I reached out and grabbed her hand and squeezed it tight as the waves roared next to us.

"Hey, Ben," she said, grinning mischievously "we should get married." Behind her smile, she looked half serious.

I laughed. "Sure, that would solve everything."

"After the trial and everything is over we could have a totally freaky wedding, a great party for all our friends and family. Wouldn't that be fun?"

"That part sounds good."

"And can you imagine what cool little kids we would have, crazy blond curly hair."

Now she was scaring me a little bit. "Kids!?" I said. I looked her up and down, trying to read her.

"Yeah," she said. "They'd be great. One with blue eyes, one with brown eyes. They'd be smart and artistic. They'll love the

Kinks and old Charlie Chan movies and we can all sing 'Were You Ever in Quebec' together as we work in a garden behind our house in the country." She was getting into it.

"Sure," I said, "That would be great. Someday. A family, man, can you imagine us with a family?"

"Yes, I can," she was smiling radiantly now. The wind gently lifted her hair from her face; the sun easing down toward the glimmering blue horizon cast a soft shine on her cheeks.

"I wish I could," I said. "There's just so much … "

"Come on, Ben, you can, it's just playing 'make pretend.' We can talk about jail or going underground or disappearing—that's all make pretend, too, now. We don't know what's going to happen. Can't we make pretend that you don't get convicted, that we find a great place to live, that we get a chance to make our own decisions about getting married and having kids." A kind of sadness crept into her eyes, small beads of tears forming at the edges.

I hated seeing her sad. "Yeah," I said, finally, "We can." I squeezed her hand again and we exchanged a serious look. "It would be an incredible party—and we *would* have great kids."

We slowly ambled back to the camp area, my arm around her shoulder, hers around my waist, clinging tightly to each other. Sydney was cooking up beans and franks with onions and tomatoes. Rusty and Herschel were ready for another epic cribbage battle.

August 15, 1970 [Clam Beach, Northern California]

Sarah was real upset when we got here. I didn't notice anything happen on the ride up from Mendocino with Sydney and Dale, but as soon as we got out of the bus, she just took off walking toward the beach, which was pretty far from the parking area. I followed after her. Low clouds hung over the water, which was an out-of-focus tumbling roar off in the distance, and a chilly breeze raised bumps on my skin. The beach was rocky and stern and told us plainly that we were north of the golden paradise where we had started. As I caught up to Sarah, we both had our shoulders hunched in to try to stay warm.

We hadn't talked much during the day's drive. I kind of spaced out, digging the magnificent redwoods we'd driven through, feeling small and awed—and lucky, too, to be in their amazing shadows.

As we walked into the salty wind, she said she'd been thinking about how she fit into the group. She felt like an intruder and didn't feel like she had anything to contribute.

Sydney was kind of the Wendy to our tribe of Lost Boys, doing all the cooking and even kind of scolding us now and then when we got a little out of control. And Sarah certainly wasn't one of the boys. She said she felt weird vibes from Mike, and Dale didn't seem to pay any attention, and Stu and Rusty just seemed distant. She wasn't pissed at me or anything, except in the roundabout way that I did have a connection to all of the others, which made me part of a club that wouldn't let her in—that's what she thought, at least. I tried to tell her that we were all trying to figure out our place in the group, but she said I couldn't understand what she was going through because I *was* connected to everybody.

Herschel was like the wise old man among us—shit, he must have been 24 or 25—and the most sensitive to the dynamics of the group. He had been in graduate school in social work at BU. And he was kind of an outsider, too, a latecomer to Montfort Street. Sarah agreed that he might be a good person to talk to. He was helping set up camp when we found him and asked him to walk with us to a nearby picnic area.

Herschel listened to Sarah's rap. I didn't say anything.

"You have to decide if you want to relate to the group as a couple or as two individuals," he said after she was through.

Herschel kind of looked like a rabbi, with his wire-rim glasses resting on his long crooked nose above his full black beard. His hair—curly and black rising up straight from his head—was a little unruly for a rabbi, I guess, but his eyes were staid with compassion. "But the reality is Ben already has an individual identity with the group because of the time he's spent with them in Boston and you're still kind of an add-on to that. There's Ben … and Sarah." He looked at me. "Does Ben sacrifice his individual identity so that his primary identity is as part of a couple? I don't know that he could do that even if he wanted to. Now, Dale and Sydney have strong individual identities, but I think their primary identity is as a couple. They go off and do their own thing, make decisions between themselves, and then announce them to the group. It's cool if that's how they're most comfortable and everyone seems to understand that, implicitly, of course, it's not as if they announced that intention, but that seems to be the way it is."

He paused and looked back and forth between us. We were sitting on benches at a picnic table, a low rolling dune between us and the beach, blocking the wind. He spoke to Sarah.

"Or do you find a way to establish your own identity, outside of being part of 'Ben and Sarah'. It's up to you. You can do it if it means enough to you. I can see that you are a strong person." I nodded in agreement. "Ben knows that, but you don't always show that to the others."

"I'm not sure how to do that," Sarah said. "Sometimes I get such strange feelings from everybody else—especially Mike. I don't think Mike likes me."

Herschel smiled. "What do you expect? You stole his best friend." Sarah shot a look at me, surprised and almost amused. "It was one thing," Herschel said, "when you were the far-off girlfriend in Philadelphia, but now you're here full time and Ben's attention is focused on you. Mike might not even be aware of it, but I see it and, clearly, you see it, too, but you just didn't fully understand where it was coming from."

Tensions between Mike and Sarah had been evident for a while but I hadn't ever thought about it like that. I mean, how could I? Two incredibly strong people that I loved and admired in dramatically different ways caught up in some kind of jealousy—over me?

Mostly, and our beach-hopping road trip had brought this out, I struggled with how to maintain both relationships, to figure out how to express the sometimes distinct parts of me that Sarah and Mike stimulated when I was with both of them. And too often, I thought as we mulled over Herschel's tidbit of wisdom, I failed all three of us. I could tell from Sarah's sadness, that I had failed her. But that also made me realize that I was as uncertain about how to fit in the group as Sarah. Maybe the difference was that I was trying to figure out how to blend the connections I felt to everybody while Sarah was trying to figure out how to make connections—and, in some ways, I was an obstacle to that. But what could do I do?

As we all gathered a little later close to the campfire in the gray dusk, everyone seemed a little down. I'm sure the relative harshness of this beach at the north end of California and the hovering cool clouds contributed but we all also were keenly aware that this great adventure was about to end and we still hadn't found a place for the next chapter.

And even more than not finding a place, it turned out as people started opening up in a way that hadn't happened before, almost everyone was dispirited because of feeling some variation of Sarah's sense of not belonging in the group. Finding a physical place, a house on some land, was our agreed-on goal, but each of us finding our psychic place within the group proved at least as daunting and as evasive a task. What was this *we* that huddled around the crackling fire on randomly arranged driftwood logs on a cold beach and how did all these *I*'s fit into it.

Stu, who usually confined his comments to his quick-witted one liners, dug circles in the sand with a short stick and finally talked about the awkwardness he felt in the divide between the couples and the single guys, which he seemed more conscious of than the others.

"Mike gets lost in his books and his bullshit theories," Stu said, smiling with the last part. "And Herschel is some kind of monk or something, just letting everything roll over him. I just feel like I'm tagging along for now until we can find a place, our place that also feels like my place where I can get to work on the land, start planting a garden." His eyes brightened as he talked about his garden. He stopped digging in the sand and looked around, serious for a change. "Shit, man, I don't want to go back," he said. "Sometimes, we just get so bogged down in group bullshit that I can't relate to and I think that gets in the way of the most important thing: finding a place. Until we get a place, this is all just a summer's fantasy trip."

"We don't have to find a place to do work, together," Sydney said. She had spread a blanket on the edge of the driftwood formation and was organizing things to cook for dinner. "That could start now. Every day, we have to get water, cook dinner, and clean up. Not glorious revolutionary work, just stuff that's gotta get done. Not everyone chips in as much as they should." She smiled at Stu and then seemed to nod toward Mike and Dale, with the same accusatory grin.

"In case you're wondering," she went on, as she peeled some onions. "I don't love being the main cook and organizer and den mother to this traveling circus." Sydney usually didn't talk a lot when we had group discussions. She'd just state her position and then listen to everybody rattle on—well, mostly Mike, Dale, Herschel and me, with Sarah and Rusty jumping in now and then—and then restating her position again. Dale enjoyed the sparring but would usually end up backing up Sydney. "I just need a little bit of order," she said, "and I don't see that coming from anyone else. And it does give me a way to fit in this group, even though I couldn't tell you what the hell we are or where we're going. But I would like a little more help."

Sarah and I exchanged looks across the fire, sharing our surprise that Sydney, too, who seemed so in control, felt some insecurities, too.

"Well, it's a little strange to say this," Sarah said, "but it makes me feel a little better to hear that I'm not the only one who feels a little out of it. Most of you had so much time together in Boston this last year … "

Rusty laughed and said, "Hey, you feel out of it? I feel like a hitchhiker you guys just picked up and I'm just going along for the ride. But I'm completely cool with that. It's been a great trip."

Sarah laughed with him. "Yeah, I get that, But I'm glad you're here, never would have learned cribbage otherwise. And I do really like everybody and feel like we're all trying, but …" her tone and expression shifted and she looked over to Mike, who was staring down at the sand just a few feet to the side of her. "Sometimes, Mike, I feel like you wish I weren't here, that you don't really like me."

Mike looked up, shot Sarah a quick serious look then looked around at everyone else with a forced smile of innocence. "Nah, man, that ain't true. I like you okay," he said, but looking at Dale, who was on the other side of Sarah.

"Herschel says it has to do with me kinda taking more of Ben's attention or energy or something. I'm sorry if that's it, but I'm not sure what I can do about that."

Mike laughed, looking at me. "I don't know about that shit." And finally, he looked at Sarah. "It is different, you know. It's different with you being around all the time, but I can dig it, and I can dig you. But … it's not like you're my new best friend just because you're hanging out with Tucker. I don't think you'd want it that way." Sarah nodded at him, matching his serious look.

"I mean, I'll try to cut you some slack," Mike said, "but the truth is, you're going to have to earn my respect. It wouldn't be real any other way. Understand what I'm saying."

Sarah grinned at him. "Sure, Mike, I understand. I hope you understand, it works the other way, too."

"That's cool." He smiled at her—and meant it, I think. He really could be sweet and he was fiercely loyal once you earned his friendship. That's one thing with Mike, you always knew where you stood. Sarah was like that, too. As different as they were, they really were a lot alike.

It got quiet. Stu subtly moved over toward Sydney and grabbed a knife and started slicing onions. Everyone looked for something to do to help, some way to physically express the underlying wish we all had for some sense of group unity that we still couldn't quite hammer out through discussion. Supper came and went and Mike and Dale did dishes and the thick coastal gray darkened to deep black. We pulled our driftwood benches in closer to the crackling, dancing fire and the conversation drifted from the challenging but refreshing revelations about our group dynamics toward thoughts about the revolution that some of us thought was coming and that we would be part of. I think it was Dale who went from raving about the amazing Jefferson Airplane concert the previous spring in Boston the night of the riots in Harvard Square after the Chigago 7 guilty verdicts came in to rapping about the nature of the revolution.

For Dale, it was a magical sort of blend of the power of rock and roll and cosmic forces beyond our understanding. We were tiny pawns in an unfathomable battle of armies of dark and light. Our role was to resist the dark and seek the light through drugs and music and celebratory living.

Mike scoffed. The revolution would be an ugly and brutal war. Billions of people would die and America, "the belly of the beast," would be destroyed by Blacks and people from all over the world who had been oppressed by the United States. "It's going to fucking happen," he said. "We just have to figure out what we can do to undermine the government and align ourselves with the right side of history, so they don't wipe us all out, too."

"Can't wait for that man," Stu said. "Where do I sign up?" Everyone laughed, except Mike. For Stu, the revolution was more about getting your hands dirty than international political forces and he loved to give Mike—Mikey the Mouth, he called him—shit.

"I'm not interested in going to war for anything," said Rusty, who was the only one among us who really knew anything about war. "Done that. It sucks. Fuck 'em."

"The voice of experience," Sarah said, and there was a collective nodding acknowledgment that Rusty's words carried a little more weight than any of ours.

The surf was crashing somewhere off in the black night behind us. Someone tossed another bone-dry piece of driftwood on the fire and it flared, bringing a hot glow to the faces of my brothers and sisters. The wind was cold. We all knew Mike was three-quarters bullshit, not so much wrong as saying things from the most outrageous view possible. I was foolish enough to try to translate that to what I thought were more reasonable terms.

"I think a lot of what you say is true, Mike. It could get ugly. They won't let go of power willingly, but I think there are ways to undermine them without going to war, to try to build a counter reality that undermines them just by its existence. Isn't that what we're trying to do?"

Sure, the silence surrounding the snaps and crackling of the fire seemed to say, that's what we're trying to do, create a counter reality. But what the fuck does that mean?

Trips into nearby small towns McKinleyville and Trinidad the next day turned up no leads on places, so we prepared to split up. Sydney and Dale were heading to Orleans to visit Sydney's cousin and then up into Oregon to see Crater Lake, next on their list of great American tourist destinations. The rest of us would go south. I had to be in Boston September 8 to prep for my trial. Sarah would go to Philadelphia and maybe school. We'd head toward Berkeley in Herschel's van, and from there Sarah and Rusty and I would try to find a ride east. We planned a stop at a campground along the Navarro River, where Stu and Mike—tight brothers despite their sometimes widely divergent world views—planned to hang out while they figured out their next step.

It's not like we had a major breakthrough around the fire that night at Clam Beach or made any kind of definite commitments about the future, but it seemed to lift the tension that had been building as our time was running out and our chances of finding a place diminished rapidly.

In a strange way, that last night together, when the underlying uncertainty that all of us felt about our place in the group had been exposed, led us to see that there was an *us* to be part of—not an *us* with clarity of purpose and a five-year plan, but an *us* defined by a shared sense of letting go, of seeking something new—and some kind of crazy love for each other. Refugees. Pilgrims. Being lost was a first step to finding what we were looking for. Nobody said anything like that out loud, and it was just a bare beginning, but, still awake that night as the fire faded and died in the cold moist wind, I couldn't help but believe that this trip was far from over.

September 3, 1970 [Urbana, Illinois]

Sarah was in Philadelphia and it was just me left in the midlands, between the collective promise of the wild and open West and the lingering lives and battles of the tired, tamed East. I slept late in my parents' basement, dawdled there, smoking cigarettes lying on the sofa bed, reliving the freedom and dreams of our vagabond summer, avoiding any thoughts of the looming trip to Boston, the lawyers and the trial, the hassle of cramming into some friend's apartment on some noisy busy street, the frustrations of waiting for Sarah to figure out how she fits into the pending chaos of my life.

I put off as long as possible staggering out into the thick humid day to find Scotty at Chins or Deluxe to drink the late afternoon away before finding Barry to smoke some hash and watch my old friends and new friends of my old friends come and go, busy in the world I left behind. It was easy now being in Champaign-Urbana because I didn't have to be anything but a memory and I could just get blasted and watch. It was only for a few days anyway.

We left Stu and Mike by the Navarro River, a beautiful spot in the woods inland from Mendocino, after a day and a night of serious partying with other folks gathered there, lots of wine and pot. They couldn't handle going back to Berkeley, so they were going to hang there as long as they could and then probably head to a farm that some people Stu knew were getting together in western Massachusetts.

Berkeley had been a trip. We slept in Herschel's van, parked outside the house where Steve had been staying. He was gone now but the rest of the folks there were still sorta friendly. There were no beds or couches available but they didn't mind if we parked outside. The money that my mother was supposed to send had arrived, which made it easier to have a good time. The second day we were there, Rusty found someone who needed a car to be driven back to Champaign—and would give him $40 for gas—and asked us to join him on the trip. Perfect, but we couldn't leave for another few days.

So we made the most of our time in the Bay Area, meeting up with some other friends from Boston; joining a protest at the San Francisco Hall of Justice for "Los Siete," some Latino kids who had been accused of shooting a cop, which got a little scary when the pigs divided the crowd and started busting people, so we split quickly; getting into a mind-blowing Grateful Dead show (almost literally, the crescendo of "St. Stephen" was accentuated by some kind of explosions, which rocked my acid-addled head) at the Fillmore; hanging out in Golden Gate Park and Marin County. One day, Herschel and Rusty and I tripped around Berkeley. Man, there were a lot of freaks doing crazy stuff. Berkeley could be cool if you had a good solid place to live with good friends and a good flow of income, but I think we were a couple of years too late to get in on that scene.

Rusty, Sarah, and I took off eastward in the early evening and drove through most of the night, finally stopping at a rest area east of Salt Lake City just after dawn. Slept for a couple of hours and then back on the road, driving up into the Rockies, into Medicine Bow National Forest, where we decided to camp for the night. It was beautiful, hardy evergreen trees growing out of rugged rock outcroppings. We passed meadows full of sheep and cows and small herds of deer as we climbed up, up, up almost to 11,000 feet at our campsite. The air was sweet and the vistas were stunning but it was freezing cold after the sun went down. Sarah and I only had one sleeping bag between us, and it wasn't working for both of us, so finally I just let her have it and put on as many layers of clothing as I could and wrapped myself in a blanket, but I was still freezing my ass off, and woke up every hour or so, hoping it would be light. Finally, of course, it was, so I made a quick fire and waited for Rusty and Sarah to wake up.

We hit the road right away, stopped at a Spudnuts—donuts just like we used to get in Champaign—in Fort Collins, full of cowboys, who were none too welcoming, then on to Boulder, where Rusty had a sister who was much older than him and very straight. We couldn't get out of there fast enough, and I'm sure she was happy when we left, too. Then we rolled into the mountains west of Denver. Man, that was a spectacular drive, rising up through the juts and chasms of the east face of the Rockies. Rusty knew some people—maybe through a Navy connection—who had a beautiful, big cabin surrounded by blue spruce and chokecherries. They welcomed us with joint after joint. We bought a couple of six packs to go with marijuana-laced spaghetti. We ate and smoked and drank until we all passed out. That was a good night's sleep. We woke to strong coffee and pancakes and more joints. Man, this kind of place would work for us, but somehow I figured those folks had more money and resources than we would ever be able to come up with. We all would have been fine just hanging out there for a few days, but we had to move on. Rusty asked them if he could roll a couple joints for the road—and he rolled two big fat ones, that we took apart as soon as we got going, rolling six smaller ones to get us through the long flat day of eastern Colorado and Kansas that lay ahead.

We got to Sarah's brother Harry's place in Kansas City about nine that night. We smoked the last of our joints after the two of them called home to talk to their parents. A few of Harry's friends were there and we had a good time, ate some more spaghetti and had a putting contest with a little golf set-up he had. I was terrible but it was funny. After a while though, Rusty and I were ready to hit the road. We were about six hours from Champaign-Urbana and the two of us just wanted to get it over with. But when I told Sarah we were ready to leave, she wasn't into it at all. She was afraid we would hurt Harry's feelings, staying such a short time, and that it would be foolish to drive all night when we had a good place to stay. I had my mind set on leaving and I was pissed because I thought she knew that and it was bogus to suddenly spring it on me that she wanted to stay. Besides, I told her, two of us wanted to leave so we won by majority rule. That really pissed her off. Just about then, Rusty came into the room where we were talking and said Harry and his friends were driving him buggy and he wanted to leave right away. Sarah agreed to go but she was pissed. I tried to make some peace on the way to the car, but she wouldn't talk to me.

She didn't talk to me, in fact, for most of about 300 miles. I was driving and she was sleeping off and on. I did try again at a bathroom stop and even half-apologized, but when I tried to explain why I was so set on leaving that just started us arguing again and she ended up crying, saying she didn't want to talk about it anymore and shut her eyes and turned away. Behind the wheel of the quiet car, cruising on the nearly deserted interstate, I had a lot of time to think about it.

Shit, how do you resolve a conflict like that? It is a drag when time and hurrying get in the way of being good to people you care about. But when you've got two opposite ways to go and you have to pick one, somebody's going to be unhappy. I knew the majority rules thing was bullshit, but I was determined to go and grabbed at any argument that made me right. We didn't fight much, so I guess we weren't very good at it—so we just stalled into unresolved silence.

Just past the Illinois border, I pulled over to let Rusty drive. Sarah woke up. We looked into each other's eyes—with the kind of sadness and regret that it was hard to find words for—grabbed each other's hand and kissed. The impasse was broken. Right and wrong seemed meaningless, it was the distance we'd allowed between us that scared us both. A stupid little argument could separate us like parents and cops and living in two cities never could. Sometimes it's the small things that happen when you're not paying attention that get you. Shit, man, it's hard always paying attention to what's going on in another person's head when you've got so much going on in your own.

We arrived at my parents' house in Urbana about seven in the morning. My mother was awake getting ready to go to work and my sisters Cary and Kim woke up to greet us. Cary told us that Stu had called from Berkeley to say that Dale and Sydney had found a house in some little town in Oregon and that he and Mike and Herschel were heading up there instead of coming east. Cary didn't remember much of the details, but she said Stu sounded real excited.

Sarah and I talked with my sisters for a little while before we had to excuse ourselves to try to get some sleep. We cuddled up close, still trying to recover from our trans-Missouri and Iowa fight, on the sofa bed in the basement.

"Oregon," I said, "That sounds pretty cool."

"Sounds very far away," Sarah said, as she closed her eyes and fell into the soft rumble of sleep.

September 15, 1970 [Cambridge]

Stu sent the letter to Jeffrey's place on Dana Street, where Sarah and I were staying. I read it first as Jeffrey kept the hash pipe loaded and lit.

Dear Tucker, Sarah, Jeffrey, and anybody else still left back there. First off, the Red Sox suck. I know that even 3,000 miles away from Fenway Park—I can smell how bad they stink from here. The Yankees may not win the pennant but they will finish ahead of the Red Sox and that's all that really matters.

But we are thinking of our Boston friends often as we swim in the river across the road, take walks in the woods behind our house, and eat wild blackberries til our bellies hurt. We think, "Why are those fools still back in the city?" Oh yeah, I know why you're back there, but get all that shit behind you and get out here as soon as you can. Take it from me, this is where you want to be.

Our place is a big white house with five bedrooms and a wood stove for heating. The nights are getting kind of cool but the days are still warm and sunny. It costs $50 a month. You heard that right! Did I mention there is a river—the Umpqua River—right across the street, where we swim every day. Naked. Are you ready to come now? We have a good spot for a garden next year near the house. The fifty acres that go with the property are mostly forest on a steep hill behind the house. We've just begun to explore up there.

We're just a little ways from the thriving metropolis of Tiller, which is basically a gas station, a store, an elementary school, and a tavern that none of us have dared to go in yet. The forest service has a big headquarters there and loaded log trucks crank by our house from early morning until the sun goes down. There are a few other freak families around here but most of the locals are keeping their distance and some are openly hostile when we go into the Tiller store or into the big city of Canyonville, about 20 miles away. No surprise—there are assholes everywhere.

Mike is heading back there soon to be around for your trial, so Dale and Sydney and Herschel and me will keep things together (while we're also having a hell of a good time) until you get here.

So get done with all that bullshit and get your asses out here. The party is just getting started.

Your unfaithful servant,

Stu

"Far fucking out," I said, as I handed the letter to Sarah. She read it slowly between deep long pulls on the pipe. Jeffrey and I were smiling like motherfuckers, happily stoned and dreaming of this promised land called Oregon.

Jeffrey had been in the same BU dorm complex as Sarah and me freshman year. He was Dale's roommate and was in the same Mickey Mouse school, the College of Basic Studies, as Mike and me and a bunch of other friends—a sort of junior college within BU for kids with decent test scores but bad grades, underachieving troublemakers is what we were. Jeffrey and I shared a small apartment for about a month before our sophomore year, during which he lived with Dale and Sydney and Walter at 1387—the neat, orderly, non-Mountfort Street on the other end of Commonwealth Avenue.

Jeffrey was tall and thin with slightly hunched shoulders. His long shiny brown hair hung back from his thin elliptical face. He smoked Camel straights and his soft brown eyes were usually streaked with red, which led him to be a frequent Visine user. When he was stoned, which was most of the time, he grinned like he knew something the rest of us didn't. And he was as fastidiously neat as I was uncontrollably messy.

Sarah and I landed at Dana Street—me from Urbana, her from Philadelphia—about a week before. I arrived dutifully early on September 8, as my lawyer had directed me ("it is imperative," his telegram had said) to do final prep for the trial. Just hours after I'd flown in and taken the MTA to Jeffrey's, even before Sarah arrived, I called Orsini's office to check in and see when they wanted me to come in. I got put through to Zinzer, who told me the trial had been postponed until October 26. He told me that was a good thing, that he and Orsini continued to believe that the longer the trial was put off, the less chance there was I'd go to prison—they hoped, or expected, I guess, that the intensity of the cop's and prosecutor's desire to make an example of me would begin to wane. Well, okay, sure. But, fuck!

That meant instead of a couple of weeks in Boston before we had some basis to build our future around, it would be closer to two months. Sarah's planned short stay to be here for the trial now extended to at least those two months.

Two months of trying to figure out where to live—Jeffrey was welcoming, but Dana Street was small. One bedroom. Sarah and I pushed his carefully arranged living room furniture to the edge of the room and slept in sleeping bags on the floor, our "bed" disassembled every morning, reassembled every night. He was a great host, making us Tasters Choice instant coffee with evaporated milk in the mornings, getting us as stoned as we wanted to be every night, with smooth blond Lebanese hashish, filling the cozy second floor space with tunes like Van Morrison's *Moondance* and a fine debut album from an English guy name Elton John, spinning his meticulously kept and cleaned albums on a great stereo. That hashish was also Jeffrey's livelihood. He dealt ounces to a network of friends built during his BU days and supplemented by new acquaintances at Emerson College, where he was still going through the motions of going to school. Sarah and I had great fun playing with the piles of cash—5s, 10s, 20s—he would bring home, shuffling it up, rearranging it, counting it. We had a lot of fun living with Jeffrey, but it was not a viable long term living situation.

Two months of trying to figure out a way to make some money to keep us going. We could play with Jeffrey's money, but neither of us was ready to go into that line of work. Shit, I certainly couldn't with my legal situation and Sarah was not into it at all. So we had to think about finding some kind of work— for a month, six weeks?

Two more fucking months of not knowing what we needed to know to try to figure anything else out. Not knowing what the state was going to do to me. What the whims of the court might be, the black-robed judge—whose commute to work on that particular morning or whether he got laid the night before could have dire consequences for my life—and the jury of my peers, when I knew that none of my peers would ever end up on any jury, especially mine. And not knowing made it easier for us not to face the fact that ultimately the real decision about us and whatever that meant and wherever it led was up to us. We didn't have to make any decisions as long as we accepted that the biggest decision was going to be made for us. Two more months—a curse and a gift courtesy of the machinations of the Commonwealth of Massachusetts criminal justice system.

Two more months before Oregon could become a real choice we had to make.

Sarah laughed at Stu's letter and passed it back to Jeffrey. She smiled at me. "Far out and far away," she said, taking the pipe from Jeffrey. Far away in all senses, I took her to mean. But she *was* smiling,

"Yeah, man, we've got to get there," Jeffrey said, when he finished the letter. "I should try to finish school, get some more money together, but man it sounds so great, I don't know … What about you guys? Will you go as soon as the trial's over?"

Sarah and I looked at each other, smiling, waiting for the other to answer, maybe just to get some new hint. Sarah spoke first.

"We'll see," she said. "The trial is just one thing"—she wouldn't even begin to allow herself to imagine that the trial could actually go wrong—"It's a big step, Oregon. We hardly knew anything about it a month ago. We've got a lot to figure out."

"Yeah, we do," I said. "But is there any doubt that that is where we want to be?"

Sarah just smiled. Jeffrey looked back and forth between us again, suddenly aware the question he had asked was not a simple one. "Yeah, it does sound just like what we need," he said. He stood up to flip the record over, carefully holding a felt cleaner to the surface as it spun, gently lowering the needle down.

Sarah was right. We hadn't really thought much about Oregon before. Even when we were tramping up the California coast, Oregon was just a misty green and mysterious place, north of what we had imagined up to that point. I had a vague sense of mountains and trees and rivers and that it was harder, somehow, and wilder than California—sort of a West Coast version of Vermont, where some of our Boston friends had sought refuge, but more so. I knew that Oregon's maverick senator, Wayne Morse, had been one of only two senators to vote against the Tonkin Gulf Resolution (the document, based on deception, that opened the door to the tragic escalation of the American war in Vietnam), that Oregon had given a strong vote to Eugene McCarthy in the 1968 Democratic primary, and that through some clever co-optation and communication the governor had diverted a potential confrontation around an American Legion convention in Portland into the woods for a groovy music festival. The revolutionary in me saw that as the establishment using our culture to squash our politics. The rock music lover side of me wished I'd been there.

Those kernels of information had given me an embryonic impression of Oregon as a place of stubbornly free spirits and rugged open-mindedness. But in all the fantasies of places we could go to get away from the madness and build new lives, Oregon had never even come up—until now.

"Clear up north of nowhere," is how Ken Kesey's narrator described Oregon in *Sometimes a Great Notion*, a novel I had discovered roaming through a funky Harvard Square bookstore. "A wild-spirited and hugely powerful tale of an Oregon logging clan," the back cover told me. I was hungry for any connection at all to Oregon, the possible world beyond the waiting and the obstacles of the East.

Kesey had blown my adolescent mind with *One Flew Over the Cuckoo's Nest*, a book my mother had decided her troubled and questioning fifteen-year-old son should read. She was always subversive in that way. The incredible fog of Nurse Ratched's world became a governing metaphor for the bewilderments of those years, thick layers of impenetrable clouds where the terror of being lost and the freedom of hiding out alternated from day to day, hour to hour. I remember one late night, driving with my bandmates asleep across a dead flat Illinois landscape, totally enshrouded in ground-hugging fog, thinking this is Kesey's fog in real life, believing that the world, the ground, the road could end right here, right now and we'd go flying off the edge. Still I pressed hard on the accelerator and drove deeper and deeper into it.

Tom Wolfe had made Kesey a counterculture hero with *The Electric Kool-Aid Acid Test*, tales of an LSD-fueled trip across the United States before there was even such a thing as hippies. But somehow *Sometimes a Great Notion* had eluded me—until now, when I really needed it.

> *It doesn't seem such an unpleasant land, for all the rainfall.*
> *It seems rather nice and peaceful, rather easy. Not as nice*
> *as California, God knows, but the weather is certainly far*
> *nicer than weather back East or in the Middle West. It is a*
> *bountiful land, too, so it's easy as far as survival goes.*

Man, what more did we need?

September 27, 1970 [Cambridge]

Dear Family,

*Howdy. Well, I'm finally employed—full time 8:30–4:30
five days a week, $84 a week. And it ain't even too bad a job. I'm
working at Children's Hospital Medical Center as a transport aid.
I go to the wards and get the kids who have to get x-rays and take
them down—and when they're done I take 'em back. It gets sort
of boring at times and you just sit around a lot, but all the people I
work with are real nice and the little kids are for the most part out-
of-sight, of course. There are some pretty messed up kids, real sick
or hurt—but my stomach is getting tougher. I didn't have to cut my
hair (I did shave before I went looking for a job) but I have to wear a
tie and a dress shirt and one of those white coats. I get a standard of
living raise in a couple of weeks, $5 or $10. Also, Sarah is working
at an animal hospital, which is right down the street (Longwood
Avenue) from Children's Hospital and she has the same hours so
we can go to work and come home together on the MTA. She is
making $75 a week so we'll do pretty good. The only bad thing is she
has Fridays off but has to work Saturday and I have both Sat. and
Sunday off.*

*We are still in Cambridge and will be until Oct. 1 when we are
going to move into an apartment with our friend Leslie and some
other people. Together, we just have to pay one person's share of the
rent, which is about $60. I'm not sure of the address. I only know
that it's near Coolidge Corner in Brookline. It will have a phone.*

*The city and all its frustrations have clouded some of the clear
visions I had attained in the country. Instead of living day-to-day as
best and as full as you can, when you get back in the city you start
worrying about where it's all leading—because cities are so damn
unnatural. In the country, things are so very clear and simple, free*

and easy. Working together with all people, loving and respecting the earth, all seem so obvious as the right way to live. But in the city, people are all locked into their closet apartments and cars and there's precious little of the earth to love.

Also, with Sarah and me, all plans stop at the trial. I want to go to Oregon as soon as the trial's over while she wants to hang around the East Coast and get married or something. She is more sure that she doesn't want to go out there right away than she is about what she wants to do. As yet, we haven't reached a middle ground acceptable to both of us. We both are very definite in what we think and we both are very stubborn. But I think that whatever happens, it'll be the best thing for us.

Mike came back from Oregon with tales of paradise. I guess the most important thing is that the people are really learning to live communally—learning to be real honest with everybody, honest to the point of telling somebody you like a lot something that may hurt them. There have been many confrontations about differences that have existed for a long time but were easier to avoid in the hectic city—things about sharing, about how people relate to each other. Hardly always pleasurable—except in the long run—but always rewarding. The revolution is alive and well in Tiller, Oregon. That's why I want to go so bad—also for the trees and mountains and the fresh air and quiet. It's a big step, I think. Both Sarah and me are afraid but she's afraid enough to not want to take it, but I'm afraid like the first time I batted in Little League: I've waited all my life for this and even though I may not be so good at first, there's no way to get good unless you do it.

I enjoyed your letter, mother. You're right about the lawyers. Something strange happens to me when I go to their office, this sense of dread kind of comes over me as I'm riding up the elevators and I have a hard time being myself. I think one of my biggest weaknesses is that I too easily accept being weak at times. So after my last humiliating meeting with them, I wrote Orsini a letter. I'll give you a capsule summary. I started by saying how important honesty was in a lawyer-client relationship and that honesty went beyond answering questions truthfully. Then I wrote about the meeting with Zinzer and Big John, the detective, not going into specifics but just saying that I felt ridiculed and that they had no respect for me as a person or my way of life. I didn't say this in the letter, but I think Zinzer wants me to feel intimidated and scared and that he and they are my only hope of salvation. I don't know if that's part of the legal strategy, to keep me humble and compliant, or just his ego trip. Anyway, then I wrote about my meeting with him (Orsini) in which—I didn't tell you this before—he asked me if I'd been using a lot of speed or heroin because I looked terrible. I just told him what I thought of "hard" drugs and the reason I looked terrible was because I'd spent the day looking for a job and trying to straighten out our apartment situation. Then I went into my philosophy about the world situation, about how this society has forgotten what it means to love the earth and our fellow man, that America was the worst beast in history, etc. and that the only solution was a revolution, a revolution that is only violent when it has to be, etc—I know you've heard all that before— and that we have to start living in new ways, etc.

It was good to get it out.

One of the guys I work with is a Jehovah's Witness and he is sure the judgment day is coming in 1975 and, according to him, no matter how good a life you have led, you will not be saved unless you accept Jesus. That somehow doesn't seem very fair. But I guess not much is, right?

There is an uproar in Boston now. A hero policeman was killed by five people who were a combination, supposedly, of campus radicals and ex-convicts, who robbed a bank in Brighton, after stealing weapons and ammunition from an armory in Newburyport. It was a needless killing, I think. They had it made and as they were leaving they sprayed the bank and a house next door and shot the cop in the back with a machine gun. They've got an incredible manhunt going on now.

Well, I'm going to close. I'll write when I know my address. Keep the faith, and I will, too.

Love to all,
Ben

October 15, 1970 [Boston]

It was a sweet pale blue day as I hustled out of Children's Hospital into warmer than usual fall weather that put smiles on the lunchtime swell of people ambling down Longwood Avenue. As always, I could spot Sarah at a distance among the crowd, a sparkle about her that set her off from the white-coated doctors or medical students, the casually dressed office workers, or even all the young students, hair a little longer, clothes a little brighter than the others. And like always, the first glimpse of her, the absolute proof that she was present in my here-and-now reality, sent a charge through me and quickened my steps.

What a treat, to break up the grind of a working day with lunch with Sarah. We worked at either end of the stretch of Longwood that ran from Huntington Avenue to Brookline Avenue and when the weather was nice, we could loll about in the soft green grass of Harvard Medical School's quadrangle, almost exactly halfway between the hospital and the animal hospital where Sarah was a receptionist. One time, we actually counted steps to see who had to walk further. She won by something like fifteen steps.

She smiled when she saw me. She looked good in her work persona. It wasn't that her clothes were that different from what she'd wear anytime—jeans and a flowery cotton blouse—but she wore a demeanor that tried to blend in. She could almost pass for a straight person, though her wonderfully wild hair was always a giveaway. My hair was still long, too. I was waiting as long as I could to cut it for the trial. But I did have to wear a dress shirt and a tie. So I was playing a kind of dress-up game myself. In a lot of ways, this was all like some kind of make-pretend game, living in the city, cleaning up for work, being who we had to be, who we were supposed to be, to do our jobs. But in that half hour we could be together in the middle of the day, we could drop character, be ourselves, refresh and revitalize to get us through the rest of the day. So besides just the rush of seeing her, there was also the conspiratorial thrill of our shared secret that we were both freaks and undercover actors in this show of normalcy.

We kissed when we met and found a spot in the grass.

"How was your morning?" I asked.

"The usual, lots of sick dogs and cats—and plenty of sick people, too," she said with a little grin. But then her expression changed suddenly to wide-eyed enthusiasm. "Oh, Ben . . . and the cutest monkey. You wouldn't believe how cute this monkey is. They're looking for a home for it." Her smile got real big and her eyes plunged deep into mine.

"What? A monkey?" I laughed. "Sure, that's a great idea."

"Oh, Ben, it's so cute and really smart, too. I played with it for like fifteen minutes on my break and I fell in love with it and it just seemed so lonely and sad in the cage when I left. Really, Ben, wouldn't you love to have a monkey? It would be so much fun."

I just stared at her for a while, chuckling. She was totally gone, smitten with this monkey. I loved the pure zest of her sudden infatuation, which totally blocked out any practical considerations, like the extreme temporariness of every single part of our lives.

"Ben, I'm serious, we could do it. We really could do it. You should come by on the way home. Meet the monkey—it's a rhesus macaque and it's just so cute. You'll see, really!"

I laughed again. "You're insane. I love you and I'm sure I'd love this monkey, but ... we barely have a place to live ourselves. Can you imagine if we took home a monkey? That would be funny, I have to admit. That might be worth it in itself."

We were living in Brookline in an apartment with three women. Our main connection was Leslie, one of Sarah's best friends from high school who had also gone to BU and was part of our tribe. She lived around the corner from us when we were at Mountfort Street. Now she was living with her sister Janice and a friends of Janice's, Anita—and us for the past couple of weeks. It was awful. We slept on a roll-out sofa bed in the living room, which meant we had zero privacy and no place to put anything. One bathroom with four women and me was a constant hassle. And Anita decided pretty quickly that she hated us and seemed to go out of her way to make the uncomfortable situation unbearable. We were already looking for a different place and had a lead on a place in Cambridge with our friend Little Eddie, the now sixteen-year-old kid who had crashed at Mountfort Street after he had escaped from the McLean mental hospital. Leslie would probably love it if we showed up at the apartment with a monkey, but it would totally freak Anita out, maybe send her over the edge.

"Could we just take it home for a night, just to goof on Anita?" I asked.

"Bennnnn," Sarah looked a little exasperated. "I'm serious. Maybe they'd let us leave it at Angell Memorial until we move again."

She looked serious. I could only laugh. "You are totally insane. Think about what could happen in the next few months." My trial had been postponed again, now it was supposed to be November 17, but my lawyers said they were hoping to put it off until after the end of the year, which would mean at least three more months in the city, before our unknown, undetermined future could begin. "We don't know what the scene is going to be like in Cambridge if we get that place. Somehow I don't think showing up with a monkey would be the best thing to do." The apartment we were hoping for was with a friend of Eddie's, Justine, a young woman he'd met through school or something. Sarah and I had met her the previous summer before we left for the West Coast. She seemed cool. The apartment was a big three bedroom on Western Avenue, right across from my sister Cary's place, and someone had just moved out, so there was just Justine and her friend Karen there now. Eddie seemed to think that the three of us could share the space of the third bedroom, which had a really big walk-in closet. Couldn't be worse than where we were.

"And this will all end at some point," I said. "And then … Oregon … or whatever. Sorry, I just don't see a monkey fitting into all that."

She got sort of pouty looking. "All that's so far away. I'm sick of thinking that we can't do anything now because of what might happen sometime … we don't even know when."

I reached for her hand. She let me take it but wouldn't return my smile. "Yeah, I know, it sucks," I said. "I'm sorry."

"We could be like Curt, my coworker, the Jehovah's Witness, who knows exactly what's going to happen and when," I said, trying to shift the mood. "And he knows exactly what he's supposed to do, save people like me. It was a slow morning today—we each only picked up three kids—so he had me as a captive audience most of the time. Some of the stuff they believe in is OK. They're against war. They don't believe in hell. But man, they do believe in laying their trip on everybody else. I try to argue with him, but it's hard when the Bible is the ultimate source of truth. It wears me out. The kids are definitely cool, though some of them are so sick and sad, but he drives me crazy and I can't go anywhere to get away—except now."

She listened as she ate her tuna sandwich, kind of sympathetic, but she wasn't forgetting about that monkey anytime soon.

It was a trip that Sarah and me were hanging out, calm, seemingly responsible working folks, on the green lawn of Harvard Medical School. This was where we had escaped to when the kids at Boston English High had attacked us when we tried to pass out leaflets about our takeover of the dean's office at BU as part of a week-long anti-military campaign.

That was in the spring of our freshman year, a year and a half ago. Sarah and I were … I'm not really sure what we were at that point … not really a couple yet, I guess, though in my mind I thought we were. We were really good friends, spent lots of time together, had slept next to each other—the closest we had come to any physical love—on the floor of the dean's office along with 150 other kids the night before we went to Boston English. But she was still getting over a recent breakup with a long-time boyfriend in Philadelphia and other guys were as eager as me to fill that spot, guys she had some interest in. I really didn't know where I stood with her and was afraid of pushing too hard.

We were together a lot in the days of the anti-military campaign. It was an exhilarating happening—focused purpose, real defiant action, solidarity—and it was cool that we were going through it together. We both were certainly into the political cause but I think my involvement was part of the reason she got so involved, and I know that having her in it, too, made it all that much better for me.

But on that morning at Boston English, things sort of blew up. Our leaflets tried to explain to high school kids why we were taking over buildings at the college, why we were against the war and the draft, which a lot of them would be facing soon. There were four of us, Sarah and me, this kid named Johnny, and our friend Luke, a leader of both SDS at BU and the anti-military campaign. Things were going okay. Then the kids started turning on us, a hundred of them surrounded us. Luke tried to talk but the kids shouted him down and then attacked us: pushing, shoving, fists flying. We got split up. Sarah and I broke out of the crowd. Johnny was on the fringe. His glasses had been broken and kids were chasing him, hitting him with limbs they pulled off of nearby trees. He eventually got to where Sarah and I were and the three of us retreated to the Harvard Medical School quad, at the top of the block above the school, the very spot where Sarah and I now sat.

Luke was still in the middle of it all. Johnny was too beat-up to go help him and Sarah convinced me that I was too recognizable and would never get through the mob. She said the kids would be less likely to attack a girl. She disguised herself a little by taking off her peacoat—the day had warmed since we had left BU that morning—and putting her hair up in a red bandana. I wanted to follow some distance behind her but she told me not to, afraid that I would give her away.

Man, I hated sitting there helpless and scared. But it wasn't long before Luke and Sarah came back smiling. Luke had fought back and felt good about it. Real raw violence was still an abstraction to most White radicals at that point, but he had swung his fists in the heat of the battle and liked it. And even better, just as the mob was about to overwhelm him, a group of Black Boston English students had intervened, giving him space

to say a few words and clearing his path out of the mob to where
Sarah was waiting. It was a triumph for him. Luke would go
on to be a leader in the Weathermen, the experience at Boston
English a turning point for him, I think. If young White radicals
would start fighting back, he and others who would form
the Weathermen came to believe, they could win over White
working class kids and be taken more seriously by the Black
revolutionaries who would be the vanguard of the revolution.
Luke later took a group of Weathermen back to Boston English,
where they lined up on the steps and challenged the kids to a
fight just to prove how tough they were—to the kids, to the
Black vanguard, but mostly, I think, to themselves.

I didn't feel any triumph or any toughness that day at Boston
English. As we walked back the couple of miles to the BU
campus, Sarah and Luke walked ahead, laughing in the spring
sunshine. I could taste how much she admired him. I couldn't
blame her. I admired him, too. Johnny and I lagged behind
in beaten and defeated silence. That's the way I remember it
anyway. I know that part of what was happening in those days
was me trying to prove something to Sarah, and I didn't feel too
good about what I'd shown her that morning.

That same helpless feeling had seized me as I ran out of the
quadrangle at Northeastern, about nine months later, the cops'
batons still flailing, the woman's blood still flowing as she lay on
the grass beneath them. But then I was in motion, the subway
tracks, its bed of fist-sized rocks, and a mass of other angry
brothers and sisters, ahead of me. I did make a stand that night
and I left that scene with a different kind of helplessness—
fighting back and getting beat, rather than simply withdrawing:
different, but I still didn't know if it was any better.

And I was still, always, trying to prove something to Sarah. After that spring of my sometimes delusional but dogged courtship, despite all my clumsiness, I did somehow move her from friend to lover, to defy her parents, to stand beside me in the face of laws and daunting uncertainties, to travel to California and roaring beaches and back, to even this—mundane jobs and an awkward rollaway in somebody else's living room. And still … and still … was I enough? Could I be enough? To take her away, really away from all this, from everything that kept yammering in our heads that we were only silly kids living a ridiculous fantasy that we would wake up from any day. How could I get her to finally say the ultimate and absolute yes?

If only it were as simple—crazy, absurd, totally insane but easy at this moment—as welcoming a wickedly cute rhesus macaque into our flux-filled lives. We both knew it was going to be a lot harder than that.

November 2, 1970 [Cambridge]

Shit, now Jeffrey, too. He got busted driving back from Albany where he'd been for his father's funeral. He spent Halloween night in jail in Otis, Massachusetts. Some "Dudley Do-Right" state trooper had stopped him on the Mass Pike in the VW bug he'd borrowed to get home before his father died.

Maybe he was going a little over the speed limit, but not much, couldn't go much faster in that car. The cop, taking note of Jeffrey's long hair and red eyes—red probably from being stoned, but also he'd just been through the grinder of his father's dying and all the family trauma around that—shined his flashlight slowly around the car. In the back seat, Jeffrey's Irish setter Josh slobbered anxiously as he sat next to a small loaf-shaped package wrapped in aluminum foil. It was a banana bread his aunt had given him as a care package for his sad ride home. But Dudley assumed it was a brick of marijuana and that he had intercepted a major drug runner. He ordered Jeffrey out of the car so he could conduct a more thorough search—a highly illegal search. After the brick turned out to be bread, he had lost all probable cause for continuing the search.

The disappointment of finding still-warm banana bread beneath that aluminum foil was quickly assuaged for Dudley when he found in Jeffrey's backpack a small wooden box with inlaid mother-of-pearl, his "traveling kit" with a few grams of pot, a small pipe, and some rolling papers—the remains of the necessities he had taken to get through an extended stint at home. So Dudley promptly took him—and Josh—into custody. Now, he had to face felony drug charges at Berkshire County Court in a couple of weeks.

The last thing Jeffrey's father had said to him before he died was "Get a haircut."

Jeffrey laughed sadly as he told the story. He sat in a classic, leather-trimmed chair in the corner of his small Dana Street apartment, keeping the hash pipe loaded and lit for us. Sarah and me were on the floor on either side of an upholstered sofa where Christopher and Sandie sat between us. They were neighbors on Dana Street and friends from BU. Christopher was also facing bullshit criminal charges, trespassing and rioting from the General Electric-strike police riots at BU last winter.

Cops attacked a group of students supporting the strike in the student union who were doing nothing but chanting at some GE recruiters who had set up there, and twenty or so kids got charged with rioting and trespassing. Students trespassing in the student union? Those charges could get Christopher ten years in prison. Jeffrey's charges also carried a ten-year maximum. And my double assaults with a deadly weapon could get me forty years.

To look at our rap sheets, we were fucking serious dangerous criminals, man, and yet …we were just kids. Stoned out, silly, music-loving, peaceful (mostly), shit, even nice(!) kids. Radical in our own different ways, but only a danger to the hypocrisy and rampant injustice of "civil" society. Man, it was all sad and absurd. Hard to know what to do besides laugh, especially as the hash percolated into our consciousness. But it really wasn't funny. How do you even think about getting from twenty to twenty-one, from a kid to some kind of adult, from this angst-filled here to some reasonable there, when what you are, who you are, how you live is criminal?

Sandie and Sarah were full-fledged coconspirators. They just hadn't been busted. Sarah had come close on Halloween night, and I'd come close to making my situation worse. We decided to go to a Yippie party at the Boston Common. It wasn't supposed to be any sort of action, just a Halloween party for freaks. Dress up in costumes, listen to music, probably smoke some dope, do some chanting and dancing—celebrating life, which is as much what the Yippies were about as disruptive actions. Sarah and I dressed like Indians in the spirit of the Boston Tea Party, a historical inspiration for the Yippies. We put our hair in braids and colored up our faces with war paint. Sarah looked cool in a short leather dress she'd found in a Cambridge thrift store.

But when we arrived at the Common, cops were everywhere, apparently already having cleared away whatever Yippies had shown up. We decided to split right away, so we just stuck out our thumbs on Beacon Street to hitchhike back to Cambridge. We got picked up by three young guys from Foxboro, who'd also come for the party and were bummed that the cops had squashed it before it could even get started. They didn't know Boston very well and the streets around the Common are crazy anyway. We ended up heading the wrong way down a one-way street and were immediately pulled over by a single cop in a patrol car. After asking the driver the usual stuff, the cop scanned the car, saw us in our costumes in the back seat and told everybody to get out of the car.

We slowly shuffled out and loosely lined up on a narrow sidewalk, Sarah and I separate from the other three. We didn't know anything about them. They could have been holding drugs or who knows what. The cop checked all our IDs and asked what we were doing. I told him that we had come for a party in the Common but it was obviously not happening so we were hitchhiking home, trying to be calm and polite. He sort of grunted and looked us all over. Then he started going off on Sarah. "How did you end up with this bunch of losers, honey? What do you think your parents would think if they saw you like this with these scum buckets." He scanned her, up and down, lingering too long on the spot where the skin of her legs emerged from the hem of her dress. "You should be ashamed of yourself. Somebody needs to give you a swift kick in the ass." Sarah stared back at him, pissed for certain.

The cop glared over at me, seemingly challenging me. He could see we were a couple and I sensed he took my eyes-down silence in the face of his insults as proof that I was not much of a man, not worthy of this woman. I don't think he had run any kind of check on me. I don't think he knew I was an (accused) assaulter of police officers with a deadly weapon. He hated my guts, held me in contempt, without even knowing that.

But if I looked at him, beyond quick, furtive glances, I'd show him too much. Too much fear, too much anger. Man, I was pissed—pissed at him, pissed at myself, helpless again as someone is assaulted by a pig—and that cop was a pig—pissed that he went after Sarah, and I didn't know how to stop him.

Both Sarah and I knew that we had to get out of there by any means necessary, we just couldn't risk doing anything that would provoke him to arrest us, so we kept our mouths shut and let him rant until a call came over his radio about something more urgent and he, suddenly and surprisingly, let us go. I don't think he even gave the Foxboro kid a ticket. He got his thrill by hassling, while ogling, a hippie chick and I guess that was enough for him that night. We split and walked to the Park Street MTA stop and rode the subway home. Neither of us said much.

Things were heavy and getting heavier, for sure, as the autumn air started to have a little bite to it and the trial got closer (we hoped, mostly) but there were good times, too. We had gotten out of the crazy apartment in Brookline and now were settling in to a place on Western Ave. in Cambridge with Little Eddie and right across the street from my sister Cary. We hung out now and then with other Boston friends who remained after last year's mass exodus. Sarah and I were still discovering the joys, mostly, of living together for real, the simple bliss of sharing our space, sharing every day together.

And Mike and his old high school buddy JT had come down from Amherst and we decided to cruise in JT's Mustang down to Marshfield for my niece Samantha's first birthday party. It was cool seeing my sister Teresa and even my borderline redneck brother-in-law Ricky and to celebrate the first of the next generation. A couple of my cousins I hadn't seen in a long time who lived nearby were there. Even though we were worlds apart culturally and the four of us had gotten pretty stoned on the trip down, it felt great to be grounded in family—both the family I had been born into and the family we were creating out of the Boston tribe, to see them mix in a natural kind of way.

Christopher and Sandie had been part of that tribe but seemed headed in a different direction now. They were both still in school, determined, unlike most of the rest of us, to finish. They planned to marry and had their eyes on some property in Vermont. As the hash high faded into a heavy mellowness that evening at Dana Street, they talked about a plan that sounded frighteningly practical—degrees, marriage, East Coast country living not far from family and the known world—compared to our communal, wild, living off the land with skills none of us had, continent-away fantasy of Oregon. I could see Sarah take careful note and find my eyes with a gently questioning smile.

November 8, 1970 [Plum Island]

We escaped the city for a few hours. Six of us, along with two dogs, piled into Patrick's parents' Olds Cutlass and the VW that Jeffrey borrowed again and headed up Route 1 to Plum Island. We smoked a couple of bowls of hash before we left and cranked up the tunes for the hour or so it took us to get there. WBCN was rocking with a new album from the Dead, a couple of cuts from The Who's *Live at Leeds*, and even some previews of a new album that Eric Clapton had made with Duane Allman. Incredible stuff, man. We did a lot of giggling and head bobbing as we cruised out of the density of the city through the gauntlet of roadside attractions in Chelsea and Revere and the rotaries and continuous indistinguishable north shore suburbs of Malden, Melrose, and Saugus. Sarah and I and Walter and his dog Abby rode with Patrick, and Little Eddie was with Jeffrey and his dog Josh. We took turns passing each other and making taunting and silly faces, kind of a contest to see who could be most outrageous. It was a startlingly sunny day and we just had to get the fuck out of the city, which had been wearing us all down. And, because Patrick, a witness for my trial, had come down to meet with my lawyers, we had the two cars available so when Walter said, "Hey, howzabout we go up to Plum Island?" We all jumped at the chance.

Patrick had been a year ahead of us in school at BU, but we got to know him during our freshman year when he lived in the same dorm complex, West Campus, as a bunch of us (Sarah, Mike, Stu, Jeffrey, Walter, Sydney, Dale, and me—what would become the core of our western expeditionary force). Then he lived down the hall from us at Mountfort Street, with roommates who were just a little bit straighter than us. Patrick hung out a lot in our apartment. We—or somebody staying there—almost always had dope, so he'd hang out and we'd get him good and stoned and then talk him into raiding the refrigerator in his apartment, which was usually well stocked. The refrigerator at #9 almost never had anything in it, except maybe some milk for Stu's morning Frosted Flakes.

Patrick was tall with black hair that was just getting good in the back and a neatly trimmed full beard. He was well read and thoughtful, a fountain of facts about almost everything. At first impression, he seemed sort of mellow and laid back, but he could get intense in a hurry. During the night after Black Panthers Fred Hampton and Mark Clark were murdered by the Chicago cops, we did a joint action with the Weathermen. Patrick and I were part of a team that spray-painted "Avenge Fred and Mark" on a huge advertisement featuring Ted Williams on the Sears Building (I said a quick silent apology to Ted before getting to work) off Brookline Avenue and broke some windows at a small branch bank on Beacon Street.

And he was the one who was with me after the shit hit the fan at Northeastern. We both picked up rocks from the trolley tracks on Huntington Avenue, but I threw mine first. I don't think he ever threw his because the undercover cop jumped me so fast after I let mine go—and everything changed.

Patrick and I had met with Zinzer on Friday, along with Mike. They were my only two witnesses, the two people I knew who had seen at least some of what happened at Northeastern. Early in the meeting, Zinzer asked Patrick if he had seen me throw anything at the cops.

"No, no, absolutely not," Patrick said quickly.

"What about the rock Ben told us he threw?" Zinzer asked him.

Patrick looked at me, confused and a little embarrassed.

"It's okay," Zinzer said. "We appreciate your loyalty, but the truth is always better, especially since we believe Ben is innocent and that the police cannot prove that the rock—not a brick—he threw struck either of the officers he is accused of assaulting. So please tell me what you really saw happen."

After Patrick finished his story, in which he said he did not see the rock I threw hit anybody—that was still a little bit of a lie—Zinzer said that he was our key witness because he could truthfully testify we had tried to keep the Weathermen and others from escalating the confrontation, that I hadn't thrown anything at the cops when they were lining the steps to the arena, and that I never had any bricks.

Mike was important because he could corroborate our attempts at peacekeeping before the police riot began, but he wasn't with me after that. His story was straightforward and he told it with firm conviction. As outrageous as Mike was in the company of freaks and radicals, he knew how to play to a straight audience. He sized up Zinzer quickly and told him what he wanted to hear.

Mike had just come to Boston for the lawyer meeting and, after a short stop at our place where we got him good and stoned with some of Jeffrey's hash, he had split right back to Springfield.

Abby the dog perked up as we started getting whiffs of the ocean. The sour, low tide, boggy smell intensified as we eased past a great oozy grassy marsh leading up to a short bridge that put us on the island. Walter—and Abby—seemed to know where we were going. We headed south past a cluster of sandy streets with gray-weathered houses and, when the scene to our east switched entirely to dunes dotted with low-lying scraggly trees, pulled into a big, almost-deserted parking lot.

The dogs both bolted as soon as the car doors opened, toward a sand-covered boardwalk path through the dunes heading to the beach. The cold wind—it was spectacularly sunny but downright chilly—coming off the water knocked us humans back a bit as we tried to follow, bracing ourselves against the breeze but still giggling.

Man, that deep clean ocean air tasted so good and, after our fifty-yard near-sprint from the parking lot, the rollicking great blue waves sparkling in the sunlight as far as our eyes could see north and south greeted us with a rolling thunderous roar. I collapsed into the almost-soft sand which had just a layer of warmth from the sun's work of this day. It felt good as Sarah, a few strides behind, collapsed on top of me, laughing and breathing hard, and we rolled together in the crusty sand. And we grabbed a quick kiss, our lips surprisingly cold, excitingly fresh.

We sat up and scrambled to a little alcove in the dunes that offered some shelter from the stiff and steady wind and watched Abby and Josh run circles around each other as Walter and Jeffrey shouted encouragement. Patrick, after surveying the beach, which was all ours on this brisk fall afternoon, came and sat beside us. Eddie, who had ambled at his own slow pace from the parking lot, also joined us, positioning himself so the rest of us completely shielded him from any wind that snuck around the edges of our little nook. He pulled out a pipe and fired up some hash.

"Man, what the fuck are we doing in the city?" he said as he exhaled and passed the pipe to me.

I took a long pull and coughed it out as I passed the pipe to Sarah. "Paying some serious fucking dues, I guess," I said.

Walter and Jeffrey caught the scent of fresh hashish smoke mixed in the ocean breeze and joined us to form a circle, as their dogs continued to run. Josh, a young Irish setter with a well-groomed long red chestnut coat, would leap every once in a while with his mouth chopping, as though he was plucking some tasty flying insects out of the air. Abby, a lean mid-sized mutt with a lot of terrier in her, mostly black with some tan highlights, chased after Josh, seemingly sort of amused by his antics. She didn't have Josh's striking looks but seemed more than a little smarter.

Walter loved his dog. We hadn't seen much of him since we'd been back in the city waiting for the trial. He lived way on the other side of Boston from us and we were all just kind of knuckling down trying to make it through to whatever was going to happen next. Walter had lived the previous year with Dale and Sydney and Jeffrey at 1387 Comm Avenue and had talked about maybe going to California with the rest of us last summer but never got out of the city. Now, he was feeling the pull of Oregon. He was short with long flowing curly dark hair and a wispy longish beard. He was quick-witted, with ready quotes from the Firesign Theatre or the latest Airplane album, played serious classical guitar, and was just off the fringe of the political movement, into this sort of mysterious spiritual stuff that I didn't really understand. He was still trying to get through school, but he was a stone freak.

"What you cats doing over here?" he said, as he claimed a spot of sand between Sarah and Jeffrey. "You wouldn't be getting high or anything, would you?" he said as Sarah handed him the pipe. "Oh, well, since you put it that way, don't mind if I do."

"So are all of you going to Oregon?" Patrick asked.

"Fuck, yes," said Eddie. "Nothing going on here. Nothing going on in Miami. Why not?"

Jeffrey chuckled, "You gonna be a farmer, Eddie?"

"Well, I'll be a farmer's best friend," Eddie said. "Stu can be a farmer. Ben could be a farmer. Sarah's got the overalls. She could be a farmer. I don't know about Mike. I'm sure he'll talk a lot about being farmer. Not everybody needs to be a farmer. You need somebody to roll the joints, right?"

"Sure, Eddie" Jeffrey said. "I think I could dig being a farmer, having our own land. I gotta deal with the stupid pot arrest before I can go anywhere though. What about you, Walter? You going?"

"I dunno," Walter said. "Sure I guess. Nothing happening here. Oregon looks beautiful. I don't know much about farming but I can cook some. I'm not sure about the company, though." He scanned around the circle. "SarahBell might be all right, but the rest of you? …" The pipe came back to him.

"And what about you, Patrick?" I asked. "You going to make it to Oregon?" Patrick was living in Burlington, Vermont, with his parents, working at the family bookstore, hanging out with his friends.

"I'll get out and see you guys sometime after you get it all figured out and set up for me," he laughed. "It's pretty mellow in Burlington now. I'll see how that plays out."

It seemed like everyone assumed Sarah and I were heading to Oregon, if I didn't go to jail, which nobody ever really talked about. Sarah didn't say anything, just grinned at the semi-jive talk going around.

As my head spun from my last long hit of the hashish, I was swept away by the whistling wind and the crashing waves, the infinite blue before me. I flashed back to our summer pilgrimage on the beaches of California, to the time before Oregon became our Mecca, before Oregon was anything to us, really, but a mysteriously green and steep place beyond the edges of our imagined world of possibilities. We were so close then and didn't know it, and now it felt so far away, a shimmering beacon beckoning from an immeasurable distance, and so tantalizingly possible—we had people there—but … but … but. Everybody, everything still came to some *but* or other.

Our tribe, our motley collective of freaks, revolutionaries, stoned-out hippies, outlaws in the eyes of America, now spanned the continent from the splashing splendor of the Atlantic that stretched out behind our clustering circle to the tiny town of Tiller, Oregon, where, the tales drifting east told us, our brothers and sister (Sydney was the only woman in the first wave) lived by the rumbling roar of the South Umpqua River, which tumbled from the peaks of mountains the likes of which none of us had ever seen and down through canyons of tall-treed drippy forests where people were scarce and a new kind of freedom seemed possible, flowing determinedly toward the ragged and rocky shore of the Pacific.

The circle that had split up, with some hope that it was only a temporary parting, at Clam Beach at the end of last summer and this circle of laughter and smoke on this November Sunday at Plum Island, together made the "we" that Sarah and I were a part of, that was the future beyond this winter, beyond Boston, beyond my trial, beyond fears and doubts, beyond every single fucking *but*. The noble and glorious Atlantic, which I had grown up next to, that had always drawn me back, that was once the road to a new world, was the past we had to leave behind, we all knew that in some way or other. The only imaginable future was to the West, in Oregon, though it was still too far away in both substance and in our heads to really know what that meant. Like the revolution. Like love. It meant something different for each of us, what we needed, what we wanted, a huge green-hued blank slate for us to color in with our lives. Oregon was our promised land, and, as we struggled and played through this slogging end of our tribe's run in Boston, we looked to each other to find the will and the way to get there.

The relentless East wind that rode the ceaseless waves knew. "Go," it said, "go West, to where your dream awaits. Doubts, be damned. You have a place to be. Go there."

November 19, 1970 [Cambridge]

Eddie was living in our closet. It was a big walk-in closet, but still just a closet, with a blanket hung in the doorway, the only thing separating our room from his space. His double mattress took up the entire floor area, even curling up against the outside wall, which had, strangely, a window that couldn't quite be closed all the way, which allowed in chilly air and even the occasional drift of snow. Eddie was really smart and more than a little crazy—and he was still a kid.

I sat on a corner of his bed, as he manipulated his pile of cocaine one more time.

"So, Ben, listen," he said, sitting cross-legged with his hair hanging down as he hovered over two uneven mounds of white powder on a mirror balanced on his lap, brandishing a razor blade in his right hand, "We can do this much tonight and the next couple of days," pointing to the smaller pile, "that still leaves me almost two-thirds of an ounce. If I sell that for $110 a gram, I'll almost make my money back, so that'll be cool, right?" He carefully put away the stash to be sold and formed four thick lines out of what was left.

I laughed, "Sure, Eddie, whatever you gotta do." The thing was, he'd started with a full ounce ten days before, for which he'd paid $2,000 on his last trip home to Miami. His plan was that he'd keep a quarter ounce for himself and his friends and sell the rest to pay for it and make three or four hundred bucks.

He was always sleeping when Sarah and I went off to work and still just lounging under his blankets when we got back at the end of the day. It was fucking cold out and his "room" was kind of cut off from the heat (even though we had a big noisy boiler in a corner of our room). Eddie didn't handle the cold well, so he'd just hang out under a bunch of covers. He didn't get out to hustle the cocaine like he had planned. Once we blew through the first quarter ounce, this recalculation became a nightly ritual before we got down to the business of snorting up the newly defined surplus.

"Seriously, Ben, it will be cool," he said rolling up a dollar bill. "I'll go over to Jeffrey's tomorrow and he can connect me to some people who I know will love this stuff. Right? It's great stuff, right?" He leaned downed and snorted one line up his right nostril, then a second line up the left. He took a couple more deep sniffs as he handed me the rolled-up bill, smiling but with remnants of concern in his eyes. "Right?"

I snorted my two lines, brushed my nose to free up any residue and inhaled deeply again. It was a startling rush, first with this sense of my brain opening from the abrasiveness of this rough powder firing into it, and then an immediate sensation of soaring, potent and powerful.

"Shit, I don't know Eddie," I laughed. "I'm no cocaine connoisseur, but it works pretty good for me. But your stash *is* shrinking, man."

"I know," his eyes were big now and confident. "But there's still plenty left. I swear, I'll go to Jeffrey's tomorrow and it will be cool."

Sarah was sleeping already. She wasn't into the cocaine and was usually totally burnt out after a day of work. We'd eat something, hang out a bit, maybe smoke a joint in the evening. Just about the time she was starting to fade, Eddie would pull out the cocaine and she'd say goodnight. So Eddie and I tried to talk as soft as we could, though sometimes we couldn't control ourselves. Fortunately, Sarah was a good sleeper.

It's not like I was a big cocaine head. I'd only done it once before Eddie had shown up with this batch. But it was a strained time for all of us. The living arrangement was weird with the three of us essentially sharing a room. Eddie didn't really have a whole lot else going on. And, it turned out, we didn't get along with our two other roommates as well as we thought we would. They made it clear it was their place where they were letting us stay—even though we were paying our full shares of rent. So, we didn't spend a lot of time out in the central "shared" living space, which meant that Sarah, Eddie, and I spent most of the time in our bedroom+closet suite. Not as bad as the sofa bed in the living room with three women in Brookline, but not that much better either.

And the fucking trial had been postponed again, now almost certainly until after the winter holidays. I was getting to hate my job, more every day. I didn't mind so much when I was working with the kids but I spent too much time as a captive audience of one for the proselytizing Jehovah's Witness coworker, and, though that had been entertaining for a while, now it was just maddening. Winter had come too early, so we didn't go out much except to go to work. I was writing papers for some BU kids to make a little extra money. I had written one about *Crime and Punishment* and *Man's Fate*, a novel by Andre Malraux about a Chinese terrorist in the early days of the revolution. I called the paper "The Humanity of a Terrorist." It's easy to dismiss "terrorists" as bad guys, crazed fanatics, but most often the impulse that sets someone on that path is a passionate empathy for people beaten down in some way or other—a marked contrast to the alienated, purposeless violence of Raskolnikov. I got into that, but then I did a paper for a snooty girl from Long Island, her final paper for her degree in political science, on the political integration of Israel—how Jews from all over the world managed to work together to create a country on top of Palestinians who were already living there. I did all the research and wrote a twenty-page paper for $50. She got an A- and she was going to get a piece of paper called a degree based on my work. She wasn't even all that appreciative. I didn't feel too good about that.

Sarah and I, in those few moments when we had any time to ourselves when we weren't burnt out, still talked circles around anything that really mattered: the trial and life after that, Oregon, marriage. We daily affirmed our love for each other and that we wanted to be together, but it seemed like we didn't even know how to talk about what that really meant anymore.

So, the late night cocaine sessions with Eddie were welcome relief from the grinding grimness of what our daily lives had become. Once he reassured himself that somehow he would make the money he needed from whatever was left, he'd lay out a couple more lines and we would talk of the wonders of life in Oregon, all the friends that would gather, what our houses would be like, the continual party that would go on around us, the music, the dope, all the amazing books we were going to write, how all that would somehow change the world.

I'd slough off to bed at two or three in the morning, nestle, totally spent, next to Sarah's welcoming warmth and sleep for a few hours before waking to face another cold day of waiting.

November 28, 1970 [Philadelphia]

The quiet hung heavy. I was in the backseat of Sarah's father's Oldsmobile. He and Sarah's mother were in the front. Sarah was back at their house.

They had taken me by surprise—Sarah, too, I'm sure—when after a pleasant nonconfrontational dinner, her father Joe had turned to me suddenly and said, "Would you take a ride with Ellie and me?" What could I say? I stammered a bit, looked at the two of them, and then to Sarah, who after a second of stunned silence, said, "What's this all about?"

"We would just like to talk to Ben … alone," Ellie said, with Joe nodding his agreement.

"Um … okay … sure," I said. Sarah started to say something, but I stopped her. "It's OK. It'll be fine." Sooner or later, I sorta knew, something like this was going to happen, some kind of showdown. I just wasn't expecting it there and then.

Sarah and I had flown to Philly—with youth fare standby tickets—for the Thanksgiving weekend. And Joe and Ellie had been extraordinarily nice to me the whole time. As we filed awkwardly out of the house toward the car, it had occurred to me that all that was leading up to this … meeting? interrogation? confrontation?

We drove about five minutes from their house, engaging in some stilted small talk about the dismal season the Phillies had had and the Red Sox's frustrating mediocrity, to a deserted parking lot of what looked like a suburban train stop. A few lights offered spots of illumination but the place felt gloomy, a setting for some creepy Hitchcock scene.

"I know this might seem ominous to you," her mother started, seeming a little nervous. I could tell she, they, had thought about this for a long time. "But we both feel like it's important for us to talk to you … without Sarah. She's so quick to stop us if we try to ask any questions or challenge you in any way. We know we have to accept that you are not just a passing fancy or hope that she will grow out of you. We can't pretend that there is not something serious between you. But …" She stopped, remembering something else she wanted to say before she got to the *but*.

"As we've gotten to know you a little bit, we understand better why Sarah cares for you so much. We can see that you are good to her, that you are smart and kind, that you care about important issues … but … you are facing serious criminal charges, you've dropped out of school, she's dropped out of school, there's talk of marriage and going off to Oregon. We're worried that no matter how much you think you love each other that you're not ready to make those kind of decisions—or that you'll make decisions that you will later regret, that could have serious consequences for you." She looked back at me, forcing a smile. She had short, dark hair that curled around her head, and a tangible earnestness about her. She wanted to like me, wanted me to be the kind of boy she'd feel good about Sarah being with. But I wasn't. She was a good liberal, a social worker at a Jewish senior center who had marched against the war. But a blond long-haired goy radical freak charged with a couple of felonies? For her Sarah?

She was done with her opening statement and ready for me to say something.

I inhaled deeply. I had written a letter to Sarah's parents after they first banned me from their house when they realized that there was something happening between us, in the summer of 1969. My letter was sort of self-righteous and lecturing, I guess, intended more to impress Sarah with my forceful rhetoric than to alleviate any of their misgivings about me. In some ways it worked. Sarah defied them to see me and gradually they backed off. But now, I knew, I had to figure out some way to talk to them, to really speak to where they were coming from. They meant a lot to Sarah, family meant a lot to Sarah. With all the big choices facing us, the less ardent opposition we had from her parents, the better chance Sarah and I had to make the decisions based on what was happening between us, uncolored by pressure from them.

"I understand your concerns," I said from my awkward position in the back seat, "and I appreciate that you have given me a chance to come to your home, to be a part of your lives. You've been incredibly welcoming these last few days. I know it hasn't been easy for you, that I haven't made it easy for you." Full exhale. "Sarah and I love each other and we both believe, I think, that love is the most powerful thing in our lives, that that's what will get us through all the uncertainty we're dealing with right now." I paused.

Her father jumped in.

"Love isn't enough," he said, bluntly, a contrast to his wife's practiced diplomatic tone. He couldn't really look at me because I was seated directly behind him, so he just kind of leaned in my direction. "Believe me. I know. There's a responsibility that has to go along with love. I love my family and that means I do a lot of things I don't love so they're safe and they have a roof over their heads and food on the table."

I moved toward the middle of the back seat, so I could look into his face. A wisp of thin dark hair hung across his forehead.

He looked tired, deep dark rings layered below his sunken brown eyes. He always looked tired to me. He owned, with his brother, a garment factory that their father had started. That business had once done well, I think, but was now struggling as they continued to pay union wages while their competitors moved factories to the nonunion south and even, recently, to places in Asia. From the little I had gotten to know him and from what Sarah had told me, it was apparent he did not love the work that had fed and protected his family.

"We understand love in ways maybe you don't. Ellie and I love our daughter in a way you won't understand until you have your own kids," he went on, a little calmer now. "And we've spent our lives trying to give her a good life and now we're afraid you two are so blinded by how much in love you think you are that you'll make bad decisions that could be dangerous for her, that could lead to her being hurt. We're worried for her—and for you, too because we can see how much she cares for you. I know this romance and love you're feeling now seems more powerful than anything but it can blind you so you make bad decisions that can lead to pain in a hurry when you have to deal with the realities of life." I could see the worry swelling in his eyes, and inside of that I could see the depth of his concern and his love for Sarah. He was right to be worried. Things could get heavy and hard for us. Was I worthy to be trusted with the fate of his daughter? Would he ever believe I could be?

I thought about the twenty-four hour scare Sarah and I had recently when her period was late: the trip to the Planned Parenthood clinic in Cambridge, the relief when the pregnancy test turned up negative. Shit, a kid, I couldn't even imagine what it would be like to have a kid now. I knew we weren't ready for anything like that. Maybe someday in our fantasy future.

"I understand that fear," I said slowly, again trying to gather my thoughts. "I hope you know that I wouldn't do anything to hurt Sarah." Just then a train came barreling through the station, not stopping or even slowing down, but its rumbling racket made it impossible to be heard, so it gave me another couple of minutes to think.

"After I got arrested … on your birthday last year," I said nodding apologetically to her father, "and Sarah came to Boston and got me bailed out, I told her I was sorry that I had made everything harder, made our already complicated relationship more complicated. I told her that I had no right to expect her to hang in there with me through all the new hassles I had brought on myself. I knew it wasn't fair to her. And she got really mad at me—not for getting myself arrested, but for doubting her. How could I doubt her loyalty, her strength …her love?

"I don't know … Maybe love isn't enough. But then maybe what we have is something more than love. Because we've been through a lot already. Been challenged and tested in all kinds of ways by some pretty nasty realities—and, still, we are together.

"I know that we are here for you to find out more about me, but one of the things I have to tell you is that I think you greatly underestimate your daughter. She is a strong, smart woman. It's not like I'm telling her what to do. We really are partners in this thing and we really are different, which sometimes makes things difficult. We don't always agree. But she always stands up for herself and what's important to her. Sometimes to the point of stubbornness. You should know that." That brought just a hint of a smile to both of them.

"We do have big decisions in front of us, once the trial is over. That uncertainty makes it hard to even talk about what comes next. And we still have some differences about what we would like to happen."

"What if you go jail?" her mother asked.

"That's the thing we've talked about the least," I said, almost laughing, but stopping, knowing that would be the wrong thing to do. "But it could happen. In some ways, it would simplify things. We'd know where I'd be living for the foreseeable future. Then, really, it's up to Sarah what she wants to do. She refuses to think about that."

"Are you scared?"

"Yes." I sighed and let that hang for a minute. "But even though this has been hanging over me for almost a year now, it still doesn't seem entirely real. I don't think I'm going to go to jail. I am innocent. But …" Another searching pause. "If I go to jail, I won't have any choice but to deal with it then. Planning won't change anything, so I'd rather think about what could happen if I don't go to jail."

"And what is that?" her father asked. He just couldn't help sounding challenging.

"Well, then it gets complicated. There's Oregon, where our friends have a house waiting for us. I'm ready to go there as soon as possible. Sarah is not so sure about that."

"And what would you do in Oregon?"

"Good question and I don't have a very good answer for you." He looked exasperated. "We'll live with our friends, grow some food, I'll try to do some writing, maybe Sarah will do something with animals, we'll try to figure out how to be part of a movement for change that isn't self-destructive. I know all that sounds sorta vague and dreamy but that's the best I can do right now. We have a place to go and friends waiting for us and that's enough for me. We'll figure out the rest when we get there."

"Why Oregon, why so far away?" her mother asked with a pained smile. It was more of a plea than a question. "I never even knew anybody who lived in Oregon."

"I know it's long way." I said, trying to be sympathetic. "Sarah struggles with that, too … I don't know … Things have been so heavy … I'm not even sure how to think about a future … my life, how do I get it to make any sense?" I knew I was flailing and the more I flailed, the more serious the looks of mounting doubt I saw staring back at me.

"I don't know … " I said finally, "I guess Oregon is about freedom. Freedom from all the negative stuff we've had to deal with in the past year. Freedom from the expectations of others and from all the ideas about what we are supposed to do. Freedom to figure out—with all those kinds of restraints removed—who we are, who we want to be, what we want to do. Right now, the things that are most clear to me—beyond my love for Sarah—are what I don't want to do. I don't want to be in school when I don't have a good reason to be there. I don't want to try to pick some career that I'll do the rest of my life just to make money. I love my parents, but I don't want to live their life, and, I'm sorry, but I don't want to live your life either. I want to go someplace where we can start fresh and I know it's hard for you—and it is hard for Sarah—but the reality that Oregon is so far away, both in our heads and in the physical world, so unknown in so many ways, makes it sorta perfect for where I am in my life right now."

Her mother tried to hide the pain in her half-smile but I could see a trace of a tear in the corner of her eye. Her father grimaced: "That sounds like a wonderful fantasy, but it doesn't make me feel any better. We all have fantasies." Joe was a talented sculptor and always encouraged Sarah in creative pursuits.

"But life is hard, you have to think practically, too. I didn't hear anything about jobs or how you'll support yourselves."

"I don't know that, yet. We're both reasonably smart and can work hard. I'm sure we'll figure out a way."

He shook his head.

"What about marriage?" her mother asked.

I couldn't stop myself from chuckling now. That was not well received. "Yeah, we talk about that a lot, too. We want to be together. And we know marriage involves a level of commitment that I think we're ready to take, but … " I had to be careful. Sarah's parents didn't know we lived together in Boston. They thought we had separate apartments. And when we talked about marriage, it was usually in terms of having a big celebration of our love and not some serious institutional sacrament that would allow us to sleep together.

"Marriage is very serious," her mother said. "It's a lifelong commitment. It forms the basis of starting a family. Do you think you two, as young as you are, and with all the question marks in your lives right now, are ready for that sort of commitment?"

Tricky stuff, because I did think Sarah and I were already as committed to each other as two people could be, but I didn't think we needed a ceremony or a license to validate that commitment. But a celebration would be cool, and I knew the formal recognition that marriage would bestow on us would mean something to Ellie and Joe—that I would be, like it or not, family then; I would be one of them.

"I think we are deeply committed to each other and what we've gone through in the past year and a half is more than what a lot of married couples go through. But when we talk about getting married, like when we talk about going to Oregon, there is always a big *if* that makes everything hypothetical. So, so far, we don't get too far past what it might be like if we got married, and if we go to Oregon … maybe because we both are afraid if we start making definite plans, the trial will not go the way we hope and everything will be turned upside down. So … we talk about it but have no real plans as of now."

That seemed to lighten the air a bit. Her mother almost made it to a full smile, like I had given her an opening she could expand on, rather than contradict. "That makes sense," she said. "Even if the trial does go the way you want—God forbid it shouldn't—I still think it makes sense to take some time to get your bearings again. That will be like a fresh start for you, not having the trial over your head. Allow things to settle down for a while before you make any big decisions."

I smiled back at her. Joe kept his gaze on his wife, not smiling, not looking back at me. I think he knew that nothing they said could change my thinking—I certainly hadn't changed his—that their only chance was to play for time rather than putting up a stout offensive against me, hoping that given enough time, Sarah would finally figure out what a loser I was and get back to her real life that I had so rudely intruded upon.

"We'll see," I said, as another noisy train rattled and rolled though the station.

December 11, 1970 [Cambridge]

It was fucking freezing and bitter dark as I walked from the subway stop in Central Square down Western Avenue. I had the usual shitty day at work and had to hustle afterward to meet Zinzer downtown. It was always a trip to go to my lawyers' office, a swank suite on the third floor of a newish concrete and glass building just a strong stone's throw from the state capitol. They sorta treated me like one of their rich clients, offering to take my coat and get me something to drink while I waited, but I definitely felt like I was behind the lines in enemy territory.

Zinzer was even kind of nice to me, different from his usual stance of trying to intimidate and scare me into subservience toward him. The trial was definitely on, he told me, and this time I believed him. January 4 was the date, just over three weeks away. All this waiting and now it was going to come crashing in on us and just like that, everything would change, one way or another. I had a split second of relief followed by a rush of terror. Really, really, really. I was going to be on trial in a big solemn courtroom with a black-robed judge and a peer-free jury, on trial for stuff that supposedly happened in the chaos of a riot almost a year ago, but really on trial for my life to this point, my not-quite-twenty-one years. Guilty or innocent? Zinzer said the DA was not willing to negotiate any sort of plea bargain that didn't involve jail time for me and we—the lawyers, my parents, Sarah and me—had been firm in saying we would not accept any deal that meant I went to jail. Zinzer told me to get a haircut and to make sure I had a decent suit to wear to court, but he also tried to be somewhat reassuring about the fate that waited me.

My head was spinning with all this shit as I shivered my way past the blocks of three-story tenement houses toward home. I passed an empty lot where they were selling Christmas trees. Christmas? This would be the strangest Christmas ever. I thought about getting a tree. Maybe that would mellow out the hard conversation I knew was coming with Sarah. The horrible waiting was over. Now, some reality—horrible or wonderful—was going to happen and decisions would have to be made. I realized I only had a dollar in my pocket, so I couldn't get a tree, which were $5 and up. But I stopped at the bodega a block from our place to buy some cigarettes.

Just as our building came into view, I was surrounded by four young Black kids. I smiled at them but they closed in on me, looking anything but friendly.

"Give us your money," the tallest one said. He was four or five inches shorter than me. None of them could have been more than twelve years old. Shit, they were kids. I laughed nervously.

"What are you guys doing?" I said still trying to smile.

"We ain't fucking around, man," another said, the smallest of the group. The words were hard, but it was still a kid's voice. It was like he was mimicking something he'd seen in a movie. "Give us all your money."

"Why are you kids doing this? What do you need money for?" I didn't even think of trying to fight my way out. They *were* little kids and the doorway to my building was ten feet away. But I was surrounded and I was a little scared, but more I was stunned that I was getting robbed by a gang of children. I really wanted to understand why children would be doing this.

"We need it for heroin but that don't even matter, man, just give us your *fucking* money," the first one said. They were all starting to look around, worried someone else would come by and interfere with their mugging. I didn't believe they wanted it for heroin but I thought they must be desperate for something.

"Look," I said, "I don't want to give you money for heroin, but here ..." I reached into my pocket and pulled out the change I'd got when I bought cigarettes. It was something like seventy cents. "This is all I've got. Really. But if you come inside ... my apartment is right here—we can talk a little and maybe we can figure out some way to help you."

The small kid took my change and the rest were staring at me like I was crazy, but they followed as I unlocked the front door and went in the building. We made it to a landing, halfway up the stairs to my apartment and they stopped following.

"What the fuck is this? Where are you taking us?" asked the tall kid.

"To my apartment, just up there," I said pointing to the door. "I just want to talk to you guys."

They all turned to head down the stairs. The little one looked back, "Fuck, no, man, we ain't doing that. You're either crazy or you think we're stupid enough to walk into your trap, either way ..." he said as they hustled out the door.

I stood on the landing for a while. I was glad they left. I really didn't know what I was going to say or do once we got to our apartment. But I really wanted to understand.

When I went into my apartment, I saw Sarah and Eddie sitting on the bed in our room, laughing. I must have looked dazed or something, because they stopped and stared at me.

"What happened to you?" Sarah asked.

"You look terrible, man," said Eddie.

"Shit, man ... these kids ... these little kids ... these four little Black kids ... just outside ... they asked for my money ... they fucking wanted to rob me." I looked back and forth between Sarah and Eddie. They were stoned and I had brought a major shift of energy into the room.

"What, Ben? Are you all right?" Sarah said, now showing real concern. "What did they do to you?"

"They just kind of surrounded me … and acted tough. It was sort of funny almost at first, they were such kids, but they were fucking serious. They said, 'Give us your money.' I didn't know what to do … I tried to talk to them … they said they needed it for heroin. Shit, I can't believe it."

"What did you do?"

"I only had a little change in my pocket. I gave it to them. I tried to get them to come up here, so I could talk to them, try to figure out some way to really help them."

"What? Ben? You tried to bring them up here?" Sarah sat up, looked hard at me and then beyond me toward the front door. "Where are they now?"

Eddie was laughing, "Ben you are totally fucking insane. What were you thinking?"

"They were kids, man, I mean, really, kids. Twelve years old, maybe." I held up my hand below my chin, to show them how little they were. "Why were they doing that? It freaked me out, man. They started to follow me up the stairs, but then they thought I was trying to catch them or something, so they split. Fuck, man!"

"Ben, really?" Sarah was pissed but still a little stoned and Eddie's laughter took some of the edge off her anger. "What the fuck?"

"I know," I said. "Halfway up the stairs, I realized that was a bad idea. Didn't know what I was going to do if they came up … but, shit, I guess it worked to get rid of them. Sorry. Man, it freaked me out."

Eddie was still laughing. "Totally insane, man, but I'm glad you're okay."

Sarah's look softened a bit now. I leaned down to kiss her. It was sweet and longer than the usual end-of-the-day kiss.

"What happened with the lawyers," she asked, reminding me of the world that existed before I was mugged.

"The trial is on. Really."

"Good," she said, a reassuring firmness in her eyes.

December 17, 1970 [Cambridge]

I talked Sarah into buying a Christmas tree. There were only a few scraggly ones left at the small lot just up the street from our apartment building—and they had cut prices. Ours only cost $3. I dragged it proudly down the shoveled sidewalk in the chilled winter dusk, as a few snowflakes drifted down around us. Sarah chuckled at my triumphant air. We were moving through the urban grit of central Cambridge but the scene stirred in me some pale genetic remembrance of my kin bringing the yule tree in from woods around Haverhill or Lexington or some other classic Yankee settlement.

Sarah had never had a Christmas tree. She'd never had Christmas. As much as getting a tree connected me to my tribal roots, it was kind of an affront to hers. It's not like we were going all the way with Christmas traditions. We didn't have any ornaments or tinsel or anything and we certainly wouldn't be doing any of the religious stuff, but still … it was a little hard for her, one more symbolic reminder of how uncomfortable her family would be about our lives together.

There wasn't really a good place to put the tree, so we leaned it in a corner of the living room, sure that our roommates would object, so we'd eventually have to squeeze it somewhere in our little room.

I felt kind of silly, looking at that dried-out skinny tree crammed awkwardly into our apartment. I realized it wasn't going to bring us any Christmas magic, some glittery grace to help us through the last few weeks of this lingering limbo. It was just a dead tree in a cold apartment.

"Maybe this was a stupid idea," I said to Sarah. We were the only people in the apartment, a rare thing. Our two estranged roommates were out somewhere and maybe Eddie had taken a cab to get burgers at the White Castle in Central Square (eight blocks away), which he did with some regularity.

"Oh, Ben, it'll be fine," Sarah said, with a tender laugh. "We'll make some ornaments and string some popcorn and cranberries. It'll be fun. Maybe even Justine and Karen will get into it."

"How do you know so much about Christmas trees?"

"It's sort of hard to avoid Christmas. Even in Melrose Park."

"Yeah, I guess," I laughed softly and put my arm around her and pulled her close to me on the worn overstuffed sofa in the living room, where we never hung out when Justine and Karen were around. I let out a long involuntary sigh.

"Oh, Sarah, what's going to happen. What are we going to do?"

"I guess we're talking about more than Christmas, now." She looked more serious but there was still a gentleness in her eye. "We'll get through the trial somehow—and then …"

"But what if they find me guilty? What if they sentence me to jail?"

She pulled away and turned so she was facing me directly. "It's not going to happen, Ben. I just know it's not going to happen." She seemed pissed that I had even brought it up.

"I know. I know you have to believe that. I try to believe that, too. I mean I do believe it, but …"

"No *but*, Ben." She was getting angry.

"There is a *but*, there has to be a *but*. We've lived telling ourselves it can't happen, but just now, just this once, let's face that *but*." She wouldn't look at me. "It can happen, Sarah. The lawyers could fuck up. The jury could hate me. We know the cops will lie. I am really guilty of one of the charges. I could be convicted. I could be sentenced to jail. It could happen and it scares the shit out of me."

She looked back. She was crying. I lose all focus when she cries. I just want to say something to make her stop. "I'm sorry, Sarah. I got all this shit gurgling inside me and I just need to talk about it … with you."

"I'm scared, too," she said slowly, wiping the tears from her face. "But I literally can't think about you going to jail … I don't mean I don't want to. I mean I can't … Really … All my thoughts, everything stops then … I don't know how to imagine it. I won't."

Those words hung heavy as we stared into each other's eyes. Sarah could be so tough, so sure of herself, even sometimes hard and stubborn, but when I cracked that shell with something I said or did, she got frighteningly vulnerable and soft. Frightening to me because it forced me to see I had some power over her, a power I didn't understand or know how to wield toward any specific purpose. But I could make her cry, could rip apart her Pollyanna view that everything would always work out for the best, get her emotionally naked and frightened—and it was that exposed and fragile Sarah I saw in the depth of her wet brown eyes.

"I know," I reached for her, just touching a tensed shoulder. She didn't move. "I'm sorry. It's a lot more fun to fantasize about a big wedding party and Oregon. But I just have to say this out loud, for me as much as you: If I am sentenced, I will go to jail. I can't do the underground thing. I'll serve my time the best I can and see what happens." She just stared at me, no real reaction. "And I know you want to be loyal and true to me, but …"

"Shut up, Ben," she said, a defiant spark returning to her eyes, as she wiped her tears with the end of her sleeve. "I get it. You said it. You're not saying anything I don't know. You'll go to jail and be a good boy. I'll be the loyal woman, waiting patiently, bringing you homemade chocolate chip cookies on visiting day. OK? Is that what you want to hear?"

I squirmed in my seat a bit, turned so I wasn't facing her directly—found myself staring at the stupid tree. "You don't have to do that …"

"Ben …" She wanted me to stop.

"No, let me say this," I looked back at her. "I'm really not wanting some kind of absolute eternal pledge. Shit, everything will change if I go to jail. You'll have to be on your own. As much as those chocolate chip cookies sound great, that's not really much of a life. What about Oregon—for you? All our friends would be there. Sarah, I don't want to lose you, that's what scares me as much as actually being behind bars, because that part just seems unimaginable. But I can and I do think about how hard it would be for us, for you. Sometimes I think maybe it would be more comforting to me if you were in Oregon, building on what we've dreamed."

Now I was almost crying, too. "I know you'll try. I know you'll want to. But it's going to be hard."

The room suddenly seemed whisper quiet. Her look softened, the mad was all gone, replaced by an intense sadness. "Sorry," I said. "I just had to say that. I understand. That's all. You don't have to say anything. I love you."

I reached my arm around her and she eased in up against me. That's the position we were in when Justine and Karen came bustling through the front door.

"Cool," said Justine, "a Christmas tree. Can we help decorate it? I think I have some ornaments somewhere in my room." It was the friendliest she'd been in weeks.

"Sure," I said. "Where do you think we should put it?" …

Fa-la-la-la-la-la la-la-la.

December 28, 1970 [Boston]

I felt sort of like a little kid, but it made my mother feel better, gave her something to do. I had no idea how to buy a suit and, besides, she was paying for it. I had taken a day off from work to shop with her for my "court clothes" at Filene's Basement in downtown Boston, a suit, a couple of shirts and ties, a pair of shoes, and some socks. I didn't own a suit. I'd borrowed a sports jacket from Stu to wear to my arraignment. But my parents and my lawyers wanted me to look decent, as straight as possible, for the trial. My mother and I both knew I wasn't going to be wearing this suit often no matter what happened, so there was no point in spending a lot of money. That's why we had stood in line with hordes of eager hyped-up shoppers to wade into Filene's Basement

It was a madhouse. I guess it's always a madhouse, but the Monday after Christmas, it was fucking insane, mobs of people everywhere, moving fast and aggressively, grabbing stuff, accumulating overflowing carts, like some kind of retail demolition derby, not for the faint of heart. I would have split right away if my mother wasn't there. We had kind of joked about the whole court clothes concept and tried to approach our mission good-naturedly.

"Man," I said stopping just after we entered, a few steps above the sprawling shopping arena, people rushing by me. I felt completely unprepared to join the combatants and looked desperately at my mother.

"It's OK," she said, steeling herself and surveying the scene. "Looks like the men's clothes are over there." She pointed to a spot about half way across the store and started heading in that direction. She looked back at me and smiled determinedly, "Come on. Let's go."

I followed. My parents had tried so hard to help me since my arrest. I know the lawyer fees screwed up what savings they'd managed to accumulate for their retirement and my younger sisters' college funds. They sent out letters to more than 100 people—their friends, my friends' parents, teachers, and other adults who'd known me in Champaign-Urbana and even New Bedford—asking for character references. The results were gratifying for both them and me. People said some really nice things about me. Some of it was fluffy bullshit, "never knew him to get in trouble" and stuff like that. But a lot of them were sincere and touching, making me feel like I'd fooled a lot of people—or that I let them down by what I had become. I know it made my parents feel good, both about what the letters said and just the fact that they had done something tangible to help me. They could check that task off their list and bundle up all the different styles of pages, handwritten and typed, and send them off to my lawyers. I couldn't imagine any of that testimony about this idealistic, well-intentioned young man these people claimed to know would have any effect on a judge or a jury, but the effect it had on my parents made it worth the effort.

I followed my mother through the throngs in Filene's Basement, but I had a hard time keeping up. She kept looking back to make sure she didn't lose me and stopped when she got to the edge of the men's department. "Do you have any idea what size suit you wear?"

I shrugged and laughed a little.

"Oh, Terry"—my boyhood nickname—she laughed, too, as she threaded her way toward the suit racks. "Here's a 38, try this and we'll go from there." There were no dressing rooms, so I had to shed my heavy coat right there in the aisle and pass it to my mother—not a simple task with shoppers surging around me.

The 38 was a little too small and the 40 a little big, but close enough to fit with some alterations. We found a shade of gray she thought was good, and then we had to chase down a harried floor worker to tell us where to go in the regular Filene's upstairs to arrange for alterations. Shirts and ties were in the same area and we made quick decisions. But then we had to really fight the crowds and navigate rows of disheveled shelves in the self-serve shoe department to find the most boring lace-up brown shoes you can imagine.

As we rode the escalator up to the main Filene's store it was like a reentry into civilization from some lawless consumerist underworld. The store was still full of people, but they moved slower, quieter, and with a common sense of decorum. After a brief wait, I was directed to a dressing room and then an older mustachioed man deftly measured and marked up the suit. I watched my mother watch, with a focused and almost happy smile. The tailor assured us the suit would be ready by Friday.

It was a costume we were putting together, a masquerade of blandness and normality for my part of innocence and contriteness. Hidden in this getup, could I pull it off? Could I fool anybody?

Finally, we traipsed out of Filene's with our bags of white shirts and boring ties and dress socks (I'd forgotten there was such a thing), calmed a bit by the upstairs experience as we passed the lines of lusting shoppers still waiting to get into the basement. Mission accomplished. The frigid air of the streets of downtown was a bracing release. We smiled triumphantly as we headed to the subway stop. I couldn't remember the last time my mother and I had spent that much time together, just the two of us. It was good. It was a therapeutic productive way to avoid freaking out that soon I would be facing forty years in jail.

We had a history, my mother and I. When I was little, I was scared of her. She yelled a lot. Now, I understood she was unhappy and it wasn't really me that she was mad at. She was a smart woman who found herself stuck in a role—mother of five kids, housewife, doctor's wife—she hated. I think it pissed her off that everybody was so excited that she finally had a male child after two daughters, an heir to the name. And it wasn't even enough for me to carry the surname: I was Benjamin Rollins Tucker III, for Christ's sake. That made me the perfect target for some of the anger she held for Benjamin Rollins Tucker, Jr. And I *was* a pretty enormous pain in the ass, even as a little kid.

Then, as I got older, when my mischievousness found some coherence in idealistic rebellion, we became allies at times both in a broad political sense and, very specifically, at home, against my father. And she found ways to put her amazing mind to work, going back to teaching, which had been her work before us kids started coming along, and now pursuing a masters degree. I couldn't say she had exactly found peace with her life, but as we had gone through the past year, I became more aware of the strong voice she had found as a woman and mother and wife.

Now, we were part of a united front with my father and my sisters with one agenda item: keep Terry out of jail. There was still much about my life that my parents disapproved of—though they sometimes didn't agree with each other on the things that were OK and the things that weren't. But they both believed enough in—or maybe they just loved—what they thought was the real me to stand up with me against the specific assault of the Boston cops and the more general mindset that was trying to crush us, us kids fighting to find ways to live that made sense to us. And, man, I was grateful for that. And I tried to show it, but sometimes I still couldn't help fighting them, reminding them that it was their lives I didn't want to live.

So, it felt good in a strangely profound way to conquer Filene's Basement with my mother. Silly, maybe, with all the big shit we had to deal with. But we did it. And it felt especially good, if only for a couple hours, to be just her son, who she was helping—and to let her.

December 30, 1970 [Cambridge]

The short, stocky barber laughed when Mike and I walked into the empty shop.

"What the hell?" he said, looking back and forth between us. "Did you guys get drafted?"

Mike and me joined in his laughter. We'd smoked a couple of joints before we left our apartment. Couldn't do this straight.

"Just about," Mike said, with his big-eyed stoned grin. "Just about, man, but not quite."

The barber shrugged and motioned toward his empty chair. "What can I do for you?"

"I need a haircut," I said with a sheepish chuckle. I hadn't had my hair cut since some time in my senior year in high school two-and-a-half years before. It hung raggedly down below my shoulders.

"Hey, that works out because it just happens that's what I do," he said. "Hang your coat up and have a seat."

I found a hook on the wall next to a calendar featuring a woman in a thin red dress sitting next to a deep red motor scooter. I sat down and smiled at Mike who was sitting in one of the waiting chairs and was shuffling through the magazines piled on the table beside him.

"So … what would you like me to do with your hair?" the barber asked me, but checking us both out. He knew we were stoned and, I think, was kind of digging it.

I sighed. "Man, I don't know … it's been a long time." He laughed again and nodded. "See … I gotta go to court … it's gotta be short, I guess, I don't know," I looked over to Mike for some help, but he was laughing at me. "I'm supposed to look kind of straight. But not like a crew cut or anything."

"Yeah, yeah," the barber said, clicking his scissors, chortling. "I understand. I can do that for you. Him, too?" he asked gesturing toward Mike, absorbed in some magazine.

"Yeah, him, too." Now, Mike looked up with a kind of mock pissed off scowl. It probably had been just as long for him since his last haircut. His reddish brown hair wasn't quite as long as mine but it was thick and even more scraggly, bulging out from his scalp in all directions, a natural curliness run amok. I felt bad that he had to cut his hair to testify for me. Shit, he'd come all the way back from Oregon, mainly, I think, because he had to testify at my trial. "He's a good friend," I said. He made a surly face at me. I laughed.

"Yeah, I can tell you guys are buddies," the barber said, as clumps of my yellow hair fell to the floor. I didn't want to look in the mirror, so I spent a long time looking at the woman in the red dress and the Lambretta scooter. I always thought motor scooters were cool. My older cousin who lived in Cambridge when we were growing up had one and he was kind of my idol for a time. And the scooter woman was beautiful in a Sophia Loren kind of way, and suggestively sexy, a little bow of gold ribbon was tied around her neck, one end hanging just above where you saw the first inch or two of the gap between her breasts.

I don't know how long it took. But finally he stood back and motioned toward the mirror. I looked silly. It was pretty short in the back and the sides, a little length on top that he kind of swept across my forehead. "Fine," I said, but I couldn't be enthusiastic. It was a step toward a surrender I'd known, in some ways, was coming for months. But there it was—tangible, physical, a different *me*—staring me down. "Thanks."

It was fun but also kind of sad watching Mike getting his hair cut. He *was* a good friend. He was stoic as the barber worked. They shot the shit while I pretended to look at *Time* and the *Saturday Evening Post.*

We paid up and bundled up for the walk back home. As soon as we were outside, Mike looked at me with a sly grin. "Man, do you know how much you owe me for this?"

"Yeah, I know … ," I said. "I'm sorry." I did feel bad. His hair was really short.

"No, I don't think you do know. I mean this is … Man, you look really funny. I never saw you with short hair before. … But, man, I can't even begin to think how you are ever going to repay me for this."

"Sure, Mike," I said. We were walking fast because it was dark and cold. "I'm sure you will think of something. And I do owe you a lot because … you think I look funny?" I looked over at him. The short hair made his bulgy eyes and thick glasses even more prominent, and his ears were fucking huge. His bulk of hair had been hiding them all these years. I laughed. "Man, I really am sorry."

"Fuck you, Tucker. I do a brotherly thing like this and you're giving me shit. What an asshole. Now, you're really going to have to do something big to repay me." He looked pissed but I know he was just busting my balls.

"You know I will."

We walked the last couple of blocks in silence. Sarah and Eddie were waiting back at the apartment, fixing some kind of dinner. I think my sister Cary was going to come over. My parents were in town but they were meeting up with a couple of my aunts. We were going to do some kind of New Year's Eve thing with family tomorrow night. Tomorrow was my last day at work before the trial. The end was beginning.

As we turned to go up the steps to my building, I patted Mike on the shoulder, "Thanks, man. It means a lot."

He looked back and smiled, soft and sincere, "It's cool, man. We've got to beat this thing."

December 31, 1970 [Cambridge]

"Happy anniversary."

Sarah smiled sweetly. "Happy anniversary," she said and we kissed.

It'd been a year ago at Mountfort Street that we first made love, with the Allman Brothers throbbing in the background.

"What a year!" I said, gently rubbing her shoulder, which yielded easily to my touch.

"Yeah … what a crazy year … it's hard to believe it all fit in one year," she said and we kissed again and she snuggled in close to me.

We'd had a mellow New Year's Eve gathering with my sisters and my parents, drank some champagne but packed it in early. We were all tired and not in a particularly festive mood. Eddie was gone, back in Florida with his family for a bit. I don't even know if Justine and Karen were there. It was utterly quiet in the apartment and the incessant whoosh of cars along Western Ave seemed off in some disconnected distance.

We eased into lovemaking. Kisses, and soft touches, and gentle strokes. So much had changed since the stumbling, hungry, magnificent passion of the year before. Shit had gotten serious in spite of all our efforts to deny and defy it. That seriousness had us stuck in Boston for the coldest winter in decades, pushed us into straight jobs, tied me to lawyers who were playing some mumbo-jumbo game with my life, made me cut my hair and hide behind a bargain basement costume—and forced us into explaining ourselves, trying to make sense of lives we were figuring out as we went. Now, we made a serious kind of love, slow and deliberate, tender and considered, conscious of the magnitude of this moment, savoring, cherishing, holding onto the blossoming euphoria as long as we possibly could. It was almost a sad kind of love, but as magnificent as any we'd ever experienced.

January 4, 1971 [Boston]

Fucking Patrick was late. He was supposed to pick us up at 8:30.

Orsini wanted me there by nine; the trial started at ten. We waited a couple of minutes past 8:30 then started running the eight blocks to the MTA stop in Central Square, me in my fucking suit and clunky court shoes and Sarah in her burgundy Saks dress and half-high heels. We were lucky that we got a subway right away and made it to the downtown courthouse by about ten after, but I looked all disheveled from the run and the worry. My parents, who were waiting, leaning against the dark paneling just inside the tall-ceilinged entrance, were noticeably anxious when we finally got there. Shitty start to what promised to be a shitty day.

I apologized to them and repeated my apology to Orsini, after my parents led us into a meeting room where he and Zinzer were waiting.

Orsini was calm as he looked up from some papers spread out on a table in front of him. "It's OK," he said, smiling warmly "We have time. I just wanted to go over a few things before we go into court. Are you all right?" His smooth baritone voice was almost comforting. He pointed to some chairs where we could sit around the table.

He had a crisp haircut and a tailored suit, polished like a lawyer should be, but not too slick. Whenever I'd met with him over the past ten months, I felt reassured, confident that I would be well-represented. Sometimes I'd leave his office and feel there was no way we could lose, that we had bought the right lawyer to beat the Boston cops. But it was rare that I got to meet with him. Mostly I met with Zinzer, the assistant, who was young and seemed to get off on scaring the shit out of me about how bad the Boston cops wanted me to go to jail. Even when Orsini was making the same point, it didn't freak me out as much. He'd make whatever legal maneuver we were discussing sound like it was just another hurdle we could overcome rather than a concrete wall that it would take a miracle to get over.

"Yeah, I'm all right now that we made it here," I said, as I tried to smooth what was left of my hair into place and took a deep breath, smiled at my parents.

Orsini smiled. "You look good. Nice haircut, good suit." He looked to my parents. When they were in the room, he usually talked to them and not me. They were the ones signing the checks.

"Today, we'll pick the jury. I think we've got a decent pool to work with. We're looking for younger people, people who don't have relatives connected to the police force, people who at least have an open mind about student demonstrations. Boston's a pretty liberal city, so I think we can find twelve people like that. Black people could be risky. They are less prone to be sympathetic to policemen, more likely to believe that the police might lie about a defendant. But … Fletcher Riley is Black, so that could negate the tendency to be sympathetic to us. We'll have to try to read any of them carefully. It's not likely there will be many in the pool." He paused and looked around at us. "Any questions?"

"What about women?" my mother asked. "I'd think they would be more open-minded." My father chuckled, nervously.

"In some cases that would be true," Orsini said. "But remember your son is accused of two violent crimes"—my mother grimaced at that. He acknowledged her reaction. "*Accused*, I said, and as much as we'd like to think otherwise, the accusation does color people's perception no matter how innocent the defendant may be. Two charges just amplify that effect. Women, if we could identify a tendency, would be more likely to be sympathetic to the victims of violent crimes. But women would probably be more open-minded about the student movement in general. So, again, it's tough to generalize based solely on someone's sex."

He looked around the room again. No one said anything. "We get six peremptory challenges, which means we can remove someone from the jury because we don't like the color of their tie or the part in their hair. We don't have to justify it. We have unlimited challenges based on cause, which means we can convince the judge that this potential juror cannot be fair and impartial, someone who believes the police are infallible, for example, or someone who says, 'All anti-war protesters should be locked up.'

"This process could take a while. There are many complex issues associated with this case. But it's very important and we're very good at it." He surveyed the room. My father took a drag from his cigarette and smiled back at him. My mother looked dark and grim. Sarah looked over to me and squeezed my hand.

"Ben, just to prepare you for what it's going to be like in there … " There was a certain amount of kind concern mixed with a bit of condescension in his tone. "You'll sit up in a dock by yourself. Mr. Zinzer and I will be a little behind and to the left of you, the jury box will be to your right, and the judge directly in front of you. You are kind of on stage and you need to be aware of that. The jury and the judge will be watching you. Even if we decide not to call you as a witness, which is our inclination at this point, you will be testifying throughout the trial by how you react to what transpires in front of you. Try as much as you can to not react, to keep a steady and stoic expression on your face. I know that will be difficult sometimes with what they are going to say about you and what you did, but do the best you can."

"Will I be able to talk to you?"

"It's a little awkward during the proceedings. If you really need to talk, let me know and I will ask for a recess." That was disconcerting. On TV, defendants are always sitting right next to their lawyers and can whisper or pass notes back and forth. Not, apparently, in Massachusetts Superior Court.

"That goes for the rest of you, too. The judge and jury will figure out who you are, know that you are connected to Ben and how you react will register with them on some level. Again, try not to react in visible ways. The prosecution is going to say some terrible things about Ben. You know that. It shouldn't be a surprise. Keep your expressions as neutral as you can. OK?"

Everyone muttered agreement. Sarah looked at me with an expression that was trying to be reassuring but came across as 'What the fuck?'"

"Are your witnesses here?" Orsini asked me. Mike and Patrick, who were with me that night at Northeastern, were my only witnesses."

"I don't know," I said. "They weren't here when we got here. Patrick was the one who was supposed to pick us up."

"That's OK," he said. "They can't be in the courtroom anyway. And they almost certainly won't be called today." He nodded to Zinzer, "You want to check to see if they are here?

"OK, that's all I have to say, unless you have any questions," Orsini said.

"Any prospects for a deal?" my father asked. I was leery about any sort of deal. I thought I had a better shot of Orsini ripping apart the cops' lies than anything that involved me pleading guilty to any charges. My father still hoped, I think, that Orsini could work some magic to make it all go away with no pain.

"No, nothing has changed with that," he said. "We'll see how the jury selection goes and how they do presenting their case. It's still possible. These situations can remain quite fluid up until the time the jury comes back with the verdict. I'll keep you informed.

"OK," he said, checking his watch, "we've still got a few minutes." He looked at me. "Go to the bathroom. Have a smoke. We'll go in to the courtroom a few minutes before ten. We want to make sure we're in our seats when the judge enters the courtroom. OK?" He smiled and gave me a firm pat on the back.

Both Sarah and I lit cigarettes immediately as we followed my parents out of the meeting room. In the hall, my mother hugged me hard, and forced a smile, "You be brave in there. Remember you are innocent."

"Sure. OK," I said and tried to smile for her. I made a quick stop at the men's room. Washing my hands and checking my hair one more time—it looked neither straight nor how I would want it, another phony lie in this multilayered false reality—it was just me alone staring into the mirror. "Holy shit, man. This is really it."

As I moved down the hall toward the courtroom, I saw a small group of people gathered around my parents and Sarah by the doors leading into it. My people: Mike and Patrick and Jeffrey; my sisters Cary, Kim, and Teresa, and even Teresa's husband Ricky; my cousin Everett, my aunts Hannah and Mary. The low-key buzz among them hushed as I approached. I was touched to see them all there, to support me, I guess. But it also felt a little like I was going to my own funeral, the way they all focused so somberly on me. Just seeing them made me want to cry, that in spite of all I'd done and all that I'd been accused of doing, these people still seemed to love me. My crimes weren't accurately reflected in the charges I was facing, but I had in words and deeds declared myself an outlaw, and now, in this very public and on-the-record forum, I would be called to account. And these people had come to stand with me.

Between me and my reckoning, I passed through this warm gauntlet of hugs and grim-faced words of encouragement.

Sarah was by my side as I pushed open the heavy doors. Whoa. A surprising number of people were already in the courtroom, spread out on the back six rows of pew-like seating. The first two rows were roped off for potential jurors, the third for family and friends of the defendant and the victims. Beyond the benches was a low, lacquered-oak railing separating the spectators from where the players of this drama would strut their stuff. Low-level bit actors, clerks and bailiffs and such, milled about, moving papers and casually chatting. The judge's bench towered over all. The room reeked of tradition and judgment, all the classic wooden fixtures polished with the patina of lives twisted and wrung out around some singular act or even a series of acts, some minuscule portion of those lives.

I realized I was blocking the doorway, so I moved toward the railing. Sarah and my parents and sisters took seats in the third row. I hesitated and waited at the gate in the rail. Orsini and Zinzer weren't there so I didn't want to go into the dock yet, but I realized that all eyes in the filling courtroom—those of the victims' families, other cops, as well as people who just got off on the legal circus—were zooming in on me. I opened the gate and moved toward the dock on my right and just leaned against its back rail. I glanced back at Sarah and my parents, sure that my expression revealed my awkward fright, but tried to smile anyway and to avoid all the looks of hatred that others now shot my way.

Orsini and Zinzer came in a couple minutes before ten. Orsini shook my hand and put his arm around my shoulder, "Are you ready for this?" There was a focused energy in his eyes. This was his time, his show. He was ready. I nodded. He motioned for me to sit down in the dock. I had to go around to the front and then through another gate to my seat. As I entered, I had a moment to scan the spectators. The room was full except for the jury rows and most of the faces were unfamiliar and unfriendly. I put on my stone face, turned around, and sat down. I realized I would not be able to look back again as long as I was in the dock. Off to my side, I watched Orsini and Zinzer and the two prosecuting attorneys shake hands and shoot the shit for a little while before they took their seats. All the bit players took their places and it got quiet.

"All rise."

And we did.

The judge was tall and thin beneath his black robe. He had no hair and wore dark round glasses. He was business-like and precise in directing the proceedings. After some introductory comments, he read the charges against me separately: assault and battery of a police officer with a deadly weapon, first of Roy Bain, then Fletcher Riley. After he read each charge, he looked directly at me and pronounced the maximum sentence of twenty years in prison and asked how I pled. After the first query, I looked over toward Orsini, who nodded. "Not guilty," I said, as resolutely as I could muster, but I could hear the quiver in my voice. I was a little steadier in my second, "Not guilty" but the judge reacted as passively as he had to the first, jotting a note on a pad in front of him.

"And do you request a trial by jury?"

"Yes," I said, again looking over at Orsini, who offered some direction while nodding toward the judge." … Yes … your honor," I stammered. The judge showed a little grin as he wrote something else down. "Very well," he said. "Let us proceed with the jury selection."

Behind me, bailiffs led in prospective jurors. The judge introduced himself, the lawyers, and me to them. I turned quickly and nodded toward them when he said my name. The judge talked about the charges and the circumstances surrounding them and asked if any of them had reasons they couldn't be impartial in this trial. One woman raised her hand and said all her male relatives were police officers. She was excused.

Then Orsini and Donnelly, the lead prosecutor, huddled next to the judge's bench, going over the questionnaires jurors had filled in advance. From this, two others were excused, one, I found out later, who'd been charged for disorderly conduct in a dispute that involved the police and the other had been arrested in a civil rights protest in the early '60s. Shit, my people.

The clerk then read off randomly selected numbers to pick the twelve people to initially fill the jury box. I studied them as they walked past me. They all looked straight to me. Mostly older, might have been one under thirty. Nine men, three women. Eleven Whites, one Black. Made me realize how much bigger Boston was than the student ghettos where I'd been playing around for the past few years, how I'd never been part of that "real" city. Except for limited contact in my occasional jobs, I hadn't been hanging with this sort of people. And now, by law, they were my peers and deputized by the Commonwealth to judge me. As soon as they were all seated the court took a lunch break.

Lunch was just a blur of uneasy small talk with my friends and relatives. I couldn't eat much of the sandwich that somebody brought me. When court reconvened, Orsini and Donnelly took turns questioning the potential jurors. They were all friendly and smiling as they asked what often seemed like hostile questions, Orsini trying to root out biases in favor of the police or against the student movement, or even just students in general.

Donnelly, pretty much the opposite, was looking for people who had had bad experiences with police or who had strong opinions against the war or in support of any sort of activism. They both identified two people who the judge agreed to dismiss for cause and Orsini used one of his peremptory challenges to get rid of someone who was clearly pro-cops but not enough so for the judge to see prejudicial bias. Alternates replaced the removed juror and after about two hours, all agreed to accept the twelve this process had left in the jury box.

To me, most of them seemed uninformed or apathetic. How could someone paying any attention in 1970 not have strong opinions about the police and the Movement and the political and cultural divide between young people and their elders? The scary thing from my position was that predisposition to believe the police or support the government was not considered bias.

I was surprised that Orsini didn't use more challenges, but he had to make a calculation on whether there might be somebody better in the pool. He couldn't just keep going until he found the ideally open-minded people. And based on the twelve people still in the box, I could see why he was skeptical about doing any better than what he had.

I was not encouraged. But the one Black man on the final jury gave me a little hope. He was probably in his mid-fifties, tall and thin with close-cropped hair and an open smile. He had answered Orsini's questions about the police thoughtfully. He respected the police but understood they sometimes went too far or made mistakes. Similarly, he handled Donnelly's questions about the student Movement with tact. He appreciated the idealism behind the Movement but was against any sort of violence. I think both lawyers thought he was persuadable.

I worked hard at being stoic in the dock, mostly focusing on the Massachusetts state flag, which hung between the judge's bench and the jury box. When the lawyers were doing the questioning, I could steal looks at the jurors, who were primarily focused on the person addressing them. I tried hard to avoid direct eye contact. Occasionally though, I got caught by a juror suddenly turning my direction. I looked back to the flag as quickly as I could. What I saw in the instant of exchanged looks from most of the jurors was a distant scrutiny, like I was of another species that they needed to assess. But with the Black man, our mutual gaze held a little longer, and there was just a hint of warmth in his eyes.

January 5, 1971 [Boston/Cambridge]

Man, it was hard not to react, sitting in the dock, listening to bullshit. The prosecution's first witness, a big bulky cop named Bennett, just told a fucking fairy tale. He was reasonably well spoken but almost nothing he said was true. I was there at Northeastern that night, but I don't believe he ever saw me. It's entirely possible he wasn't there that night, that he was just a designated testifier because he could string a few intelligible sentences together. He certainly didn't see me do the things he said I did.

He said he was on the steps of the Northeastern auditorium facing out at the crowd of demonstrators on that cold January night when Hayakawa was supposed to speak. He said he saw me in the crowd, me, specifically, in my dark blue pea coat and my long blond hair, among a thousand other kids massing and generating that crazy frenzied scene. He pointed at me and told the prosecutor he was sure it was me. He said he saw me rise above the crowd, standing on one of the benches in the quadrangle in front of the auditorium. He said he saw me throw a brick toward the police line on the steps. He said he saw that brick fly from my hand to the face of Fletcher Riley. He said he saw Fletcher Riley's face ripped apart as Riley crumpled in pain onto the hard granite steps. He said, at the same time, he watched me climb down from the bench and try to disappear into the crowd that was retreating from the lines of policemen who were now charging the mass of protestors. He said he was able to keep sight of me and chased after me across the quadrangle.

None of that was true. I never climbed on a bench. I never touched a brick. I never threw anything at the cops on the steps. I was part of the retreating crowd, but I never felt like someone was chasing me in particular. When I slowed my retreat because two cops were beating the shit out of a girl behind Patrick and me, they never stopped to come after us. But other cops were coming toward us so we didn't think we could do anything to help her. But it never seemed like anyone was chasing *me*.

Going on, he said he saw me cross Huntington Avenue and join the couple of hundred demonstrators who had regrouped across the street from the quadrangle and at that point he lost me in the crowd. But, fortunately for him and the police, an average Joe do-gooder citizen, just casually hanging out on Huntington in the middle of a riot, saw me throw another brick at the reorganized police line that was advancing on the demonstrators. That brick was the one that struck Officer Roy Bain, Bennett said. At that point, the good citizen waded into the crowd of angry militant protestors and grabbed me and promptly turned me over to my personal Inspector Javert for that evening, Officer Bennett.

What a neat story. And it gets a little murky because there are elements of truth mixed in with the fairy tale. I did cross Huntington Avenue with Patrick and joined with the remaining protestors. Patrick and I were looking for Mike and our other friends. But I don't believe Bennett saw me because I don't believe he was chasing me because I know I didn't stand on a bench and throw the brick that broke Fletcher Riley's face.

I did throw something at the police line across Huntington Avenue but it was a rock that fit easily in my hand—I never touched a fucking brick that night. Patrick and I each picked up a rock from the MTA tracks when we crossed the street. And I did see it hit a cop, who I guess was Bain. I saw it hit him in his right cheek. I saw blood come from his face and saw him go to his knees where he was held up by other cops surrounding him. A guy close to me yelled, "Good shot, brother," and that's when I felt somebody grab me. But I'm near certain that he was not a civilian, that he was a Red Squad goon, an undercover cop. And his turning me over to uniformed cops was not quite as tidy as Bennett described.

Orsini, I think, did a good job in cross-examination. He forced Bennett to describe the general chaos of the scene, the uneven light in the quadrangle, the difficult sight lines once he was down off the steps, with cops and panicking kids moving helter-skelter around the quadrangle, between him and the singular person he had decided to pursue—that is, me, according to him. Orsini led Bennett to admit that there were lots of objects being thrown out of the crowd of kids on Huntington Avenue toward the police line and that the crowd was both dense and unruly. Orsini never called him a liar. He was kind and sympathetic, emphasizing what a difficult situation it must have been for the police. But after getting Bennett to vividly describe a situation where it would be nearly impossible for any human being to identify one specific individual as throwing specific objects at other specific individuals and then pursuing that culprit, Orsini calmly asked him again if he was still sure it was me that had done all those things. Bennett, of course, said he was still sure, but there was just the slightest hint of diminished certainty in his response.

I tried to discreetly watch the jury during Bennett's testimony. Their eyes, for the most part were fixed on the witness, so I could sneak peeks every once in a while, just shifting my eyes without moving my head. They were hard to read.

Somebody must have told them to avoid expressions or maybe they did take their responsibility for impartiality seriously. But I could see subtle indications that they liked Orsini, that his empathetic approach to cross-examination seemed to work. I think he succeeded in planting an element of doubt in their minds, especially with the one Black man on the jury. He was seated in the middle of the first row of jurors, so he was close and centered in my view. Something about his demeanor and the openness I sensed in his eyes led me instinctively to see him as my best hope. Even during the testimony, we exchanged quick glances, and though I couldn't say his look was friendly, it was searching, like he was really trying to figure out what kind of person I was. The others who caught me looking, would quickly turn away.

I felt slightly hopeful after Bennett's testimony.

The prosecution's second witness was Bernard Russell, a tall Black man, who I think was the Red Squad cop who grabbed me. Only that's not who he was on that day in Suffolk Superior Court. He was, in court, under oath, just a man who happened to be walking down Huntington Avenue on January 29, 1970. He got caught up in the crowd of demonstrators who had massed on the sidewalk across from the Northeastern quadrangle after they had been pushed there by the charging Boston police. He saw a kid with long blonde hair throw a brick—again with the fucking bricks—toward the police line coming across the avenue toward the crowd. He saw that brick hit a police officer, who he later found out was Roy Bain, and he, out of some deep sense of civic duty, grabbed the kid and managed somehow to pull him out of the crowd of angry militant demonstrators and turn him over to the first uniformed cop he saw, who, amazingly, turned out to be Officer Bennett.

And, yes, he saw that young man in the courtroom. He pointed resolutely at me.

Fuck!

I lost my best hope on the jury as Russell's story unfolded. I watched despairingly as the eyes of the Black juror showed the slow transition from open inquiry to something on the other side of a shadow of a doubt. One cold look in my direction told me that. At the same time, I could see the rest of the jury falling under Russell's spell.

Of course, something quite different actually happened that night. After he tried to grab me, I broke free and ran through and out of the crowd toward an alley, sure I could outrun him with my lead-off hitter's speed. The alley is where that alleged civilian shouted, "Stop or I'll shoot," with something that looked like a gun peeking out of his pocket. After I stopped, he handcuffed me before yanking me back toward Huntington and turning me over to the uniform cops, one of whom may or may not have been Bennett. What an amazing stroke of luck, that this good citizen decided to take his handcuffs with him for his evening stroll down Huntington Avenue. He was no fucking civilian. He was a motherfucking Red Squad pig. And he was a hell of a convincing liar.

And what does it matter? They lied. I lied. I can say their lies were bigger, more dangerous. A higher percentage of their version of the events of that evening were lies. Maybe 80–85 percent. In my story to my parents, to my lawyers, to my sisters, to Sarah's parents, to anyone but Sarah and my very closest friends, I left out one single detail. I told them all I threw a smaller-than-fist-sized rock toward the police line but in the chaos and with the man grabbing me from behind, I never saw where it went. But, in truth, I did see it hit the cheek of a cop, who I believe was Roy Bain. I saw the blood. I saw him fall. I felt pretty damn good about it for a second or two, felt like I had scored a little payback for the girl getting beaten down in the quad, like I had finally struck a physical blow against the brutal violence of those cops and all pigs and the imperial US of A—until the man tried to grab me. But I left that part out. How could anybody ever prove that I saw what happened to that rock? How could anybody ever prove that my rock was the one that hit Bain—especially when they kept saying it was a fucking brick. I didn't even see any bricks that night. So I had a lie that could have been true within the reality of that night. Their lies were a concocted distorted story. Doesn't that make my lie less egregious than theirs?

It didn't matter. Their big, coordinated lies were more believable to the jury than my almost true story, which I never got to tell. And if there was some kind of magic truth-telling pill we all had to take, and all the facts were laid bare, I still come out guilty of one count of assaulting a police officer with a deadly weapon, though my real weapon was a lot less deadly than my weapon in their fairy tale. Maybe ultimately, I could have gotten off on that technicality. But we never got that far.

After Russell's direct testimony, the court recessed for lunch. Orsini and Zinzer went into the judge's chambers with Donnelly and his assistant. Sarah and I and my parents went into a meeting room to wait for them. Somebody brought us sandwiches that we all sort of picked at. Not much talk among us after we first sat down and I said, "Man, what a liar. I know he is a cop. No doubt about it."

We waited an excruciating hour. I smoked cigarette after cigarette. We all knew it was lost.

Orsini was smiling when he came in. Just another day at the office for him. "We've got a deal," he said. "No prison." My mother let out an audible gasp and tears rolled down her face. My father exhaled, "Thank God." Sarah squeezed my hand and tried to smile. I withheld any reaction. I knew there was more he had to tell us. "What's the deal?" I asked.

"You plead guilty and you'll get probation, two or three years. Fletcher Riley and Roy Bain won't insist on jail time for you. I think it's the best deal we can get, Ben." I think he wanted me to be happy.

"Plead guilty to both charges?"

"Yes, that's the deal, Ben."

"But I know I'm innocent of one. For sure."

"It doesn't matter, that's the deal: plead guilty to both or the trial goes on. I think Mr. Russell's testimony hurt us a lot. If the trial goes on and you're found guilty, you almost certainly will go to prison."

"You know most of what he said was a lie."

"I could possibly impugn some of his testimony on cross-examination but he was a powerful witness for them. A civilian stepping in to help the police."

"He's not a civilian."

"Whether he is or not, the jury believes he is."

"What do you think are our chances are if we keep going?" I asked. Zinzer was looking at me like I was crazy. My parents had matching expressions of deep concern, sort of supportive but scared, too. Sarah's eyes were firm. I don't know what she was thinking but I knew she was with me.

Orsini was calm. "I'm too confident in my abilities to tell you it's hopeless, Ben. But it is a big risk. If I said, it was 50-50, is that enough of a chance for you to take that risk, to go to prison?" He gave me a long look, then looked to my mother, then my father, then Sarah, then back to me. "I think our main objective when we took this case, with the police animosity toward you and the political climate, was to keep you out of prison. This deal accomplishes that. You can put this behind you and get on with your life." He smiled at Sarah.

It got quiet for a while. I thought of the last hard look from the one man on the jury—a man whose name I couldn't even remember—who I had imagined was on my side.

"He's right, Terry," my mother said, solemnly, reaching her hand across the table and putting it on top of mine. "I don't like you pleading guilty to something you didn't do, but this would give you a chance to get a new start." My father gestured his agreement.

I took a deep breath and looked to Sarah. Now, she had a real smile and met my eyes with that crazy unconditional love that showed me a way that things could be okay. The complicated mess I had made of my life suddenly for just that moment seemed simple. Prison or Sarah? Some distorted need to prove something to somebody or a chance to make a life with this beautiful woman who had stayed when I had given her so many reasons to go.

"OK," I said. I looked around the room at everybody and got sort of teary again, finally resting my gaze on Orsini. I tried to muster something approaching a smile. I just felt so wrung out. "Thanks," I finally said to him.

Things got a little chaotic as we headed back into the courtroom. Our expressions must have told the family and friends waiting in the hallway that something had happened. Each of us had a little circle of our supporters around us, and tried to whisper the news that we'd made a deal to them. I talked to Mike and Patrick and Jeffrey. Mike looked pissed. Shit, he and Patrick, all cleaned up and short-haired, had sat outside in the hall the whole time because they were witnesses and weren't supposed to hear other people's testimony. But he was pissed because he didn't trust Orsini or the judge to live up to the bargain. He was thinking my biggest fear, but I stopped him when he started to say something. "Man, I've got to do this," I said and turned to make my way into the courtroom.

The lawyers from both sides were laughing and chatting when I took my seat in the dock. We all rose as the judge entered. He gaveled the court back to order. He said he understood that I had decided to change my plea and asked me to take the witness stand.

"Is it true you wish to change your plea?"

"Yes, your honor."

"And how do you plead?"

"Guilty, your honor."

"Are you making this change of plea of your own free will and having been fully informed of the potential consequences?"

"Yes, your honor."

"I want to make sure you understand the implications of what you are doing. You are admitting you are guilty of two felony charges of assault and battery of a police officer with a deadly weapon, each of which carries a potential penalty of twenty years in prison. A guilty plea means the trial ends and we will move on to sentencing. Do you understand that?"

"Yes, your honor."

"Did you commit these crimes?"

I hesitated. "Well …" I looked over toward Orsini and saw his face tighten. "I think it's a good chance I committed one of them." Orsini very subtly moved his head from side to side and his eyes were yelling at me.

"You don't know?" the judge said. "And your new plea was guilty to both charges. Are you having second thoughts about that?"

Orsini was now calmly freaking out. I scanned the gallery, saw Sarah, my parents, my sisters, my cousins, Jeffrey, Mike, and Patrick, all the friends of cops who hated me, all of them staring hard, wondering what the fuck was about to come out of my mouth. I just fucking wanted to tell some reasonable approximation of the truth, to be judged for what I really did, for who I really was.

I looked at the judge, hovering above me in his black robe and his radiating somber authority.

Fuck.

"No, your honor. I plead guilty to both charges. I committed both of these crimes."

"Are you sure."

"Yes, your honor."

"Very well, please return to the dock."

The court adjourned for the lawyers to confer with the judge about sentencing, which should have been just a formality since the deal called for me to get probation and no jail time. I don't know if Orsini showed them the character-reference letters, seventy-five or eighty of them, I think, my parents had spurred people to write. All the people who wrote letters made me feel good, but also kind of humble and sort of guilty. A few did it as a favor to my parents, but most did it because somehow I had made them think good things about me: teachers, parents of my friends (including some old girlfriends), the disciplinarian at my high school, shit, even a retired cop. A lot of them sent copies of the letters they sent to Orsini to my parents. I didn't recognize the positive, naïvely idealistic kid they described. I knew I wasn't him anymore.

I don't think they spent a lot of time with those letters because after about an hour, they called us back in the courtroom. Fletcher Riley took the stand and did say he trusted the court's judgment as to whether or not I should go to prison. I watched him closely as he testified. He never looked directly at me. I don't know if he knew that the story about me hitting him with a brick was a fable. Probably not. Most people if they tell or hear a lie often enough, they begin to believe it, at least on some level of their consciousness. Deep down, I think, most liars retain some link to the truth that can reveal itself under the right circumstances, that maybe even actively pushes against the false reality that they try to maintain. But, as far as I knew, Fletcher Riley had never told any lies about me. He was a victim, got his face smashed while trying to do his job. That's all I really knew about him. And as he testified, he sounded like a decent man, capable of forgiving me even if I had been the one to throw whatever it was that hit him. I was sorry our lives were forever linked by his pain and other people's lies.

Roy Bain declined to testify during my sentencing.

Finally, the judge asked me to stand and face him.

"Having received guilty pleas from you on two counts of assaulting a police officer with a deadly weapon, I hereby sentence you to two 18-month terms at Walpole State Penitentiary to be served consecutively."

Above the sudden tense buzz in the courtroom, I heard my sister Cary cry out and I heard Mike shout, "Motherfuckers!" As the volume of reaction increased, I turned to stare down Orsini, calculating what sort of effort it would take for me to jump over the rail to grab the son of a bitch.

The judge banged his gavel to quiet the court.

"Those sentences shall be suspended in lieu of three-years' probation. If the defendant successively completes this period of probation with no further criminal activity, this court will then entertain an action to dismiss these sentences."

He gave me a very serious look. "Do you understand the terms of this sentence?"

"Yes, your honor."

"Very well. I hope you will take this opportunity to redirect your life in a more positive direction."

"Thank you, your honor."

"This court is adjourned."

That night, Sarah and I met up with my parents and sisters and some of my cousins for dinner at my Aunt Ruby and Uncle Nathan's place in Cambridge. My aunt served goose, probably a goose my uncle had shot. It was the first time Sarah ever had goose. It was kind of a celebration, I guess, but I didn't feel all that celebratory. I drank a lot of wine. My father drank a lot, too, and showed the beaming smile and overly hearty laugh of the early stages of his drinking, when he was actually fun to be with, before the incoherence and belligerence set it. My mother was off duty in monitoring him, allowing herself to be happy with the specter of her son in prison behind her. I loved seeing them let loose after what I'd put them through.

Why wasn't I happier? I could be sitting in a cell in county jail, waiting to be transferred to the state penitentiary. Right at that very moment. Instead, I was surrounded by people who loved me, who had supported me, celebrating my freedom.

Maybe I knew I didn't deserve it. I hadn't stood up and offered some kind of principled defense: I committed a crime because there were bigger crimes being committed around me, the immediate crime of police brutality, using unnecessary violence to control a crowd of mostly passive students. My violence was a response to the greater and more oppressive violence of the cops. And our presence there in the first place was a response to the society-wide crime of repression of Blacks and Hispanics as represented by Hayakawa, the focal point of our protest. And that crime came in the context of America's criminal culture of international imperialism, as being demonstrated daily in our devastating onslaught against the people of Vietnam. My crime was not some isolated act of a mixed-up kid but part of an international struggle against greed, intolerance, and horrific violence.

But, like any true description of what happened at Northeastern that night, in a small skirmish of that global battle, none of that ever made it into the trial. Because I was too scared.

As we toasted round the table in my aunt and uncle's elegant home in a tony section of Cambridge and talked speculatively, dreamily, of some future in Oregon or Sarah and me getting married, I knew that if I were Black or poor, that if I didn't have family ties reaching into the elite circles of Boston's legal fraternity, if my parents weren't willing to mortgage their future for me, if I truly lived the principles that came so easily out of my fucking mouth, that I would be on my way to prison for a long time.

I was enormously relieved. I was painfully humbled by the love of my family and friends. I was somewhat reluctantly grateful for—and deeply conflicted about—the privileges I had. But happy? I just couldn't quite get there that night, but the wine made it easier to laugh with the others.

January 10, 1971 [Cambridge]

My mother and I were in her rental car, circling the long block around our apartment building. She had picked me up at a bakery a few blocks away, where I got a bag full of pastries for the summit meeting that was about to unfold. Now we just had to kill some time so Sarah could show her mother and grandmother around "her" apartment before we showed up.

"I don't like this one little bit, Terry," my mother said, both her voice and her expression stern. "If Sarah needs to lie to her parents, that's her choice, but I don't like having to play along with it, becoming part of the lie."

"I know. I'm sorry. I don't like it either. We just gotta get through this and then … "

"Yes, and then what? Blazes, Terry, it seems like you just keep having these things you just have to get through and what the truth is and what you want always seems to get pushed to the side." She saw a parking place around the corner from our building, so she pulled into it and turned the car off.

"Do you even know what you want?" There was an odd mixture of contempt and concern in the way she looked at me.

"I want to go to Oregon … with Sarah. Soon. I know that, but … "

"What about marriage?"

"Sure, I'd be okay with marriage, if we can do it simple and soon. It's not like I think that would change what Sarah and I have, but if it makes it easier for her to go to Oregon and easier for her parents to accept, then sure—and it could be a fun gathering for our friends and family."

"Oh, Terry, sometimes you can sound like such a nincompoop for such a smart young man. Marriage is serious, a commitment. It's not a lark."

I let that hang. It was cold in the car. It was quiet for a while.

She reached across the front seat to stroke my shoulder. Her expression softened. "I'm sorry. I know you've been through a lot and you just want to get all this behind you. But don't forget you have a say in what's going to happen."

My mother had stayed on after the trial to visit with her sisters in Marblehead and Scituate. Sarah's mother and grandmother Lena had flown up for the day. We were all about to gather in our apartment to discuss our future. Man. Just five days ago, it was a black-robed judge and twelve good citizens of Suffolk County who held my fate in their hands. Now I had to make some kind of case to these three women, four counting Sarah. Sarah and I were still not quite settled on exactly what it was that *we* wanted. Oregon was definitely a destination … at some point. For me, it was as soon as possible. For Sarah, it was after she had figured out a way to make it easier on her parents that she was moving 3,000 miles away with a now officially convicted felon.

Marriage? Would marriage make it easier or harder for her parents? There was, in theory at least, a permanence to marriage that might be scary for them. But the other side was that marriage also meant a commitment that perhaps could change me into the kind of son-in-law they had hoped for, someone worthy of their daughter. Sarah and I mostly talked about marriage as a celebration. Between us, we knew that the past year we had lived through and survived, a trial by trial, had affirmed our commitment to each other and that a legal certification of that was just something to show other people.

Sarah's mother, Ellie, had really tried to find a way to accept me. She was fundamentally a peacemaker … up to a point. She was fiercely against me at first. That fierceness came from a deep devotion to her family and steadfast resistance to anyone or anything that threatened it. But as Sarah and I endured one test after another, her devotion to Sarah began to counterbalance her opposition to me. I was on the edge of being part of that family she was so fiercely loyal to. This gathering in our apartment was, I suppose, a negotiation of a peace treaty that would allow me in. But I knew that treaties usually meant some sort of surrender. And after somewhat meekly evading the state's efforts to put me in prison, I wasn't too keen on much more surrendering.

Sarah's grandmother was the unquestioned matriarch of the family. A powerful personality, she had lived a colorful life, engaging in a number of borderline dubious entrepreneurial endeavors (not-quite pornography, pencils without erasers, balloons with the occasional hole) while raising four daughters with her husband, Sam, who ran a produce wholesaling business on the docks of Philadelphia. His working hours were the middle of the night to breakfast time, which meant he slept most of the day. Sam had died three years earlier, right before Sarah and I started hanging out. Lena was born in the United States to immigrant parents and had an old-world flare in her accent and expressions and worldview, but a touch of the elegance befitting a matriarch.

I would have loved to put her together with my grandmother, my mother's mother Anna, my last living grandparent. She was a Yankee patrician through and through, born into New England manufacturing money that was mostly squandered through bad investments during the Great Depression (an uncle committed suicide over it). My grandfather died at forty-nine and after my grandmother had finished raising her kids on her own, she had married into money and a lovely New Hampshire estate called Stonehouse Farm. She always carried that near-aristocratic air. Culturally, she couldn't be further away from Lena, but the two shared a toughness that was not a commonly recognized characteristic of women of their generation. They took charge of their families out of necessity and operated with a remarkable degree of independence and self-sufficiency. Both raised strong-willed women—my grandmother had three daughters to go along with one son. And both could drive their daughters crazy with their freely offered and strongly judgmental advice.

After an initial awkwardness, I think they would have gotten along great.

For some reason, Lena had always been nice to me. Maybe she didn't take me seriously as a suitor to Sarah at first. Maybe something in me being a rebel or outsider appealed to the mischievous side of her, which showed itself in some of her business activities and expressed itself in her playful, unpolished laughter. She was tough on the nonconformists in her own family, but always showed a warmth toward me, which was welcome in the midst of the chilled reception from most of the rest of Sarah's family.

We were gathered in a circle drawn by the central sofa and some dining room chairs arranged around a low coffee table in the living room where Sarah and Eddie and I hardly ever spent any time. We had told Eddie to get lost for the day and made sure that Justine and Karen would not be around. We had stashed most of my clothes at my sister's across the street and securely hid any other evidence of me. It was always kind of cold in the apartment, with a stale smell that having critical visitors made me much more aware of. It was never a homey-feeling kind of place, which only added to the discomfort all of us were feeling—except maybe Sarah's grandmother, who had the least emotional investment and maybe the fewest preconceived notions about how she wanted this to go. It was all just awkward and strange. I lit a cigarette despite the involuntary looks of disapproval from Ellie.

We danced around the central questions for a while, as we picked politely at the pastries, engaging in introductory banter and expressions of relief at the results of the trial.

Ellie asked thoughtful questions about what my probation would mean, if it would restrict our options, with, it seemed clear, the unspoken hope that it might prevent us from going to Oregon in the near future. I repeated my lawyer's answer to that: if we wanted to move out of state, we'd have to get permission from the Boston probation office and my probation would then be transferred to our new location. He didn't foresee any problems in us getting that permission.

Which got us to Oregon.

"Why do you want to go to Oregon?" Lena asked, with the inflection on *Oregon* making it sound equivalent to Siberia or Uranus, someplace so far out of her consciousness that it was an absurdity to even consider. "Have you ever been there? Do you know anything about it?"

I held back. I'd gone over this with my mother, with Sarah's parents. I'd been making the case to Sarah ever since we got the first letter from Stu, with tales of our awaiting homestead in the promised land of Tiller. I was curious to hear her answer to her grandmother.

"Our friends are there," she said. "They've told us all about it. It's beautiful. It's near a river and they have a garden. They have a house with room for us. I know it's far away, but it's a chance for us to try to be self-sufficient, to start a farm and have animals— and to do it with our friends, who are a special group of friends, maybe it's hard for you to understand."

"We know what it means to have friends," my mother said, curtly. "We've all had special friends." She looked to Ellie, who nodded.

"What do you know about farming and animals?" Lena asked, *farming* and *animals* getting the same treatment as the fantasyland of Oregon.

"We can learn," Sarah said, undeterred by my mother's terseness or her grandmother's skepticism. "Our friends have already started. We spent time together last summer in California and started trying to figure out how to live and work together." I loved hearing Sarah being an advocate for Oregon. "We're young. I don't really want to go back to school. We don't really have anything holding us here right now. It's a beautiful place where we already know people. We can try. Maybe, probably, it won't be forever but it feels like we need to give it a try."

Yay, Sarah.

"It's a chance for a new start in a new place and this seems like a perfect time for us to get a new start," I added, just to lend a voice to Sarah's argument.

"What about marriage," Ellie asked, looking first at Sarah and then at me. "Are you thinking you'll get married before you go?"

Now, Sarah deferred to me.

"Sure, we could get married," I said, sort of chuckling. From the instant looks of varying degrees of disapproval from the four women surrounding me, I knew quickly that was not a good way to respond. Sarah's facial reaction was sort of an amused annoyance: you could have done better than that. My mother's was a continuation of the exasperation she'd expressed in the car. But she held her tongue. Lena and Ellie showed deep concern.

"Do you want to get married? It's not a joke," Lena said, direct, to the point, a style her granddaughter had inherited. Marriage, she knew something about.

"Sure. Yes. I know it's not a joke. I mean …" and I searched for words. The right words were complicated because of the overarching lie that Sarah and I were not living together, had not been living together since we headed west to California the previous summer. We'd been living like a "married" couple for more than six months, sharing our money (and lack of), our bed, our anxieties and dreams, farts and snores. I could have said, "we feel like we are already 'married' and committed and if you want us to sign some papers and have a party, well, sure." Or I could have just said, "yes" and left it at that. But I couldn't.

"I'm as committed to Sarah as I could ever be. I love her and I think, I know with how she has stuck by me for the last year, that she is committed and loves me, too. Marriage would be some formal recognition of that and a chance for our family and friends to celebrate it. Yes, I'd like to do that. But, I believe our lives together—this bond we want to certify and celebrate—will really be in limbo until we get to Oregon. We've already spent this fall and winter, hanging on, waiting for the trial, which kept getting delayed. I'm ready to get on with our lives.

"Yes, I want to get married—in a simple way and soon."

"Well, a wedding's not a simple thing," Lena said.

"We have a lot of family that we'd want to be a part of it, and I'm sure," Ellie said, looking at my mother, "you would want to have people from your family there, too. That doesn't happen overnight." She smiled at me.

My mother smiled, a little tensely, back at Ellie. "Yes, of course, we have family that we would want to be there. But I think we're getting a little ahead of ourselves. They're so young," she looked from Ellie to Lena, who nodded agreement. "They've just been through this difficult year, with their backs against the wall. Sarah's loyalty through all that is admirable and may be the basis for a successful long-term relationship, but," she glanced at Sarah, then me, then fixed her gaze back on the two older women, "they're so young."

She was talking as though Sarah and I weren't in the room. "My son talks about marriage like it's just some party for their friends. As hard as this last year may have been for them, the focus on the trial has sort of kept them from the real world. Marriage is hard. It's work. It's a commitment. Maybe this is real love, but I don't think they fully understand or are ready to make the sort of commitment that a successful marriage requires. I say, let them go to Oregon, live with their friends, try to start a farm, and see what happens. They've got plenty of time to get married later if things work out."

Wow. My mother was in her take-no-prisoners stance, brutal honesty, maybe as a reaction to the lie we had forced her to be a party to. I liked her proposal. The truth was, going to Oregon with Sarah as soon as possible was more important to me than getting married. But she was being incredibly condescending and dismissive of Sarah and me. Shit, we were too young? I don't know exactly how old she was when she married my father but she couldn't have been that much older than we were. I was almost twenty-one; Sarah had turned twenty a few months earlier. Lots of people get married at that age. How many of those had been through what we'd been through? Would my mother have been so cavalier about one of her daughters moving across the country to live, unmarried, with a recently convicted felon? She did know, as Ellie and Lena did not, that we had already lived together for half a year. It was almost like she was taunting us with that knowledge: you want to play the innocent, young couple, well this is how that plays out.

Maybe she had just soured on marriage. I was keenly aware of the difficulties that she and my father had been going through for years. They both seemed to live in regret for the lives they had ended up with and the other was always the closest and easiest thing to blame. And she was not thrilled with the husband my oldest sister, her only child to be married at that point, had chosen, young, just about the age Sarah was now.

Whatever her motivation, she had brought the conversation to an awkward stop. I lit another cigarette, the sound of the match striking and my first deep inhalation filling the charged silence.

"I got married very young," Lena finally offered, "younger than these two." She raised her eyebrows over a soft smile and looked to my mother, kindly asserting her elder status. "It wasn't always easy. But we had a good marriage for almost fifty years. It depends. Are they ready? How do I know? How do you know? But if they're determined to go off to this Oregon place together, it seems like they should get married first."

"A year ago, I would have said that, too," my mother answered, her tone softer and more measured now, maybe a bow to Lena's seniority. "But now, after spending a year in terror that Ben"—my real name sounded funny coming from her—"might end up in a prison, I don't worry so much about appearances. Kids are doing that these days, living together before they get married"—careful, Mum—"and I think it maybe makes sense. Learn about each other, what it's like when that first rush of romance subsides, and then decide if you want to make the commitment of marriage."

"This is all happening so fast for me," Ellie said, easing her way into the conversation to which Sarah and I were now curious spectators. "I can only imagine how hard this year was for you, Alice, and the relief you must feel now. And I know Ben and Sarah have been thinking about what their future might be for a long time. But … now … Oregon … marriage? I agree with Alice, marriage is a serious commitment, but so is moving to Oregon together, to a place you've never been, not really even sure what you'll be doing. I think maybe we all need to take a deep breath, let the relief of the trial being over settle in, and give it some time before making any serious decisions."

"That's not going to happen, Mom," Sarah said, quickly, resolutely. "Ben and I have been giving it some time for months. We're ready to get on with our lives. We're going to Oregon." She smiled firmly at her mother, and turned with the same look toward mine. "And we want to get married."

"Yes," I said. "I don't have a job anymore." Children's Hospital had let me know that I shouldn't come back after news of my conviction was in the newspaper. I hadn't mentioned my arrest and pending trial when I applied. "We … er, Sarah has already given notice on this apartment. Boston is done for us. And our next stop is Oregon." I looked at my mother, "Yes, we're young but we're planning on being together for a long time and it seems like an appropriate time to celebrate that with our family and friends, so we want to go to Oregon married. And we want to have some kind of party to celebrate that."

So there it was. Somehow it took our mothers from their very different perspectives telling us what we ought to do, for both of us to finally get to a firm mutual declarative statement of what we wanted. I didn't like the way my "get-to-Oregon as soon as possible" position sounded coming out of my mother and Sarah reacted the same way when her mother turned her "what's the hurry?" stance into a prolonged stalling tactic. And it was Lena, with her distance from the mother-child dynamics who asked the right questions and maybe unconsciously, maybe brilliantly, steered us to this resolution that was now clear to all. In this awkward gathering in this inhospitable setting, Sarah and I had found again our common voice, and, it felt at least in that moment, we had taken back control of our lives. Neither the faceless state or the love-wrinkled faces of those who thought they knew what was best for us were directing us anymore. For the first time in a long time I cherished the truth I first heard from Abbie Hoffman: Today is the first day of the rest of your life.

Now it was about details. When? Sarah said she liked to have an outside wedding. Her mother said that would probably mean June. No. Okay, not outside. I'd like to head to Oregon by the end of February. That would be hard, her mother said, we really do have a lot of family that needs to be there. Well, let's try and see how soon it can happen, Sarah and I said, and the wedding can be as big as you want as long as you can pull it together in a reasonable time frame—and we can invite our friends.

We were, now, engaged, fiancés, it seemed. Funny words to us, other people's ways of approaching this commitment of a couple, of lovers, that we would bend toward our own particular magic of being together. No getting down on a knee. No ring. It was on that big flat rock at the end of the beach in Mendocino last summer where Sarah and I had first talked about marriage, a wild fantasy in response to a group discussion about whether or not I should go underground, not even going back to Boston for my trial. Neither of us was keen on the prospects of life on the run, and we just started riffing on what it might be like to throw a big party and call it a wedding.

That dream of a celebration imagined on a California beach, when everything—both terrible and wonderful—seemed possible, had been nurtured, tested, tried on as antidote to the nagging fears of months of dreary waiting. Now it was becoming glisteningly real. Marriage and Oregon. Our lives once again in gear.

March 13–14, 1971 [Philadelphia]

My father was my best man. How could I choose among my best friends, my brothers? Mike had come back from Oregon and cut his hair to testify at my trial—and spent the entire time sequestered outside the courtroom. As far as I knew Stu was keeping things going in Oregon, getting ready for the new wave of pilgrims that would strike out on the trail after our wedding. But … he showed up in Philly totally unexpected. He deserved best man status for that alone. And Scotty and Barry were just as good of friends and they'd loaded into the Sensations mobile—a band van that still bore the name of the previous owners—with a bunch of other Illinois brothers and sisters for the cruise to Philly and had camped out at Sarah's aunt's house, spread over couches and floors, wherever they could claim enough space to curl up. They were all my "best" men. It's not like we were doing a traditional wedding. Sarah didn't have a maid of honor or bridesmaids or anything like that.

I knew it would mean a lot to my father, where Stu and Mike and Barry and Scotty wouldn't give a shit one way or another. Besides, my father had earned it after what we'd been through in the past year. He even earned it the morning of the wedding. The night before, at the Holiday Inn where we were staying, I showed him and my mother the "suit" I was going to wear. It was actually a costume from a theatrical rental place, featuring a 19th century-looking brown long coat that came with a top hat, an Abe Lincoln outfit (the coat reminded me of something the Kinks might have worn in their *Kontroversy*—my favorite album—phase). My father didn't object so much to it being a costume, but he freaked because it didn't fit me at all. It was way too big. So we got up early to try to find a tailor open on a

Saturday. Then we frantically dashed off, taking a cab to a funky looking shop halfway across Philadelphia. The tailor was old, spoke in a thick German-sounding accent, and was none too impressed with the garment we asked him to alter. But my dad kept buttering him up and hinting at a big tip, so he did the job—and fast. I think my dad paid him thirty or forty bucks to fix up my $10 rental costume. As much as he was acting kind of freaked out, I knew he dug taking charge and helping me out and I was only too happy to let him.

Yeah, Sarah and I were getting married. What a trip, man. Somehow, Sarah's mother had pulled a formidable wedding together in a couple of months—secured a hotel ballroom, a caterer, and a dance band. Invitations to 200 or so went out on time. Sarah bought a fraying gray Victorian dress from a thrift store and her mother hired a seamstress to rebuild it, a good match for my retailored $10 costume.

As I stood before the "altar"—a two-level platform under an umbrella-like *huppah*—next to my father, in the gleaming clean ballroom now filled with ribbon- and bouquet-lined rows of neatly aligned white seats with freaky friends and formally dressed relatives, I marveled as Sarah came down the aisle toward us with her father. She shined in her stunningly gray, full, pleated dress with hand-stitched adornments running up the bodice to cream and coral lace rising to embrace her graceful elegant neck. Her hair draped on her shoulders like an untamed stole, and she wore a crown of ribbons and soft pink roses, with streamers of gray silk flowing through her hair and down her back. She was the "altogether beautiful" bride of Solomon, chiseled by an ancient tribal history. She was the outrageous sensual freaky flower child, who had so patiently taught me love in quiet rooms and loud and dangerous places. She was Sarah, granddaughter of Sam and Lena, Moishe and Rachel, daughter of Joe and Ellie, and sister of David and Harry, product of Melrose Park, Cheltenham High, and Boston University's wild West Campus, barely twenty years old—and she was coming to tell this little gathered portion of the whole wide world that she wanted to be with me—forever. Wow. It was a big deal after all.

The two months leading up to the wedding had been a frantic, buzzing blur. We cleared out of the Western Avenue apartment as quickly as we could. Eddie went home to Miami with plans to come up for the wedding and then head to Oregon about the same time we did.

We went to Philly for a while to help with some of the initial wedding planning—guest lists and the like—and for me to be introduced to Sarah's sprawling family at an "engagement" party. We had to keep putting things in terms that straight people could relate to. Her father had helped me look the part of a fiancé by buying me some fashionably hip clothes, not my style at all, but he was kind in trying. So, with my hair still court length and these foreign clothes, I was as ill-at-ease in how I looked as in how I felt to suddenly be on the inside with Sarah's family. I knew and liked a few of her cousins who were about our age, and Lena was sort of looking out for me, but, man, the waves of relatives came in an onslaught. Besides just being Sarah's future husband, I was a curiosity, a blond-haired goy who had caused considerable consternation to the Stein family. Who knew what stories, real or fanciful, had made their way through this intricate, tangled web of relations? I found myself stuck to the floor about seven feet inside the front door of the Stein's modest cottage-like home, surrounded by the people flooding in, each explaining in great detail how they were related, which always triggered stories that all of them had obviously heard hundreds of times and people would correct each other and go off on new tangents that would be interrupted by some new person entering the circle and sending the conversation off in some new direction. I was in the eye of this raw loudness: exuberance, hearty laughter, people talking over each other, firm hugging backslapping familiarity, real warmth and deep shared affection, with the occasional raised eyebrow telling me that there was more to that particular story that I might get to hear later. I was lost in it all, like a musical neophyte hearing only cacophony in some possibly brilliant classical symphony. I craved a cigarette and nursed a straight bourbon I tried to keep refilled from the modest liquor offerings, which fortunately were not far from where I stood. I don't know that anybody else was drinking.

My family, even when we lived in Massachusetts, close to most of my aunts and uncles, was never like this—or not that I saw. I do remember, when I was very young and when my parents were still relatively young themselves, summer gatherings at a family home in Rye Beach, New Hampshire, where there was a gaiety among the adults, mythologized in family lore in the phrase, "How arhhh ya? Glad to see ya. Let's have a paaahty." But that was a distant time. Typically, at Thanksgiving, about the only time we mixed with our extended family, the generations were separated, with the kids being kids off where they could not be seen or heard and the adults gathered in a quiet room, always seeming restrained, smoking and sipping at their highballs. And since we'd moved to Illinois eight years before, we hardly saw our extended family at all.

But I made it through that party with a new appreciation of just how thick and deep Sarah's family was. It made me more conscious of how thin the connections in my family had become—and sad about that. But it also scared the shit out of me that I was now a part of this loving loud dissonant tribe, more convinced than ever that I could never live in its midst.

A few weeks after the engagement party, Sarah and I went to Springfield, Mass., for Mike and Paulie's wedding. The fact that Mike and Paulie were getting married was totally insane. If you tried to conjure up a human being that was the diametrical opposite to Mike, it would be hard to do better than Paulie. She wasn't small physically, about the same height as Sarah, somewhere around 5 foot 3, and a little stockier, but she always seemed small next to Mike, who was a notch over six feet but always carried himself, with his swagger and bluster, like a bigger man. Paulie had a soft, round face with wavy honey brown hair down to her shoulders, and a twinkle in her eye when she showed her unaffected smile and let loose an unexpectedly guttural laugh. She was shy with a sweetness and innocence about her, things no one would ever say about Mike, and sometimes she seemed incredibly spacey, off in some other world.

In some ways, their situation was not that different from what was happening with Sarah and me. Mike wanted Paulie to go to Oregon with him and whether it was for her or for her parents, getting married seemed to be a necessary step for that to happen. But Mike was the least romantic person I knew and he never talked about this deep love—or whatever it was—he had for Paulie, unlike me talking about Sarah all the time. And her parents hated him even more than Sarah's parents had (past tense, maybe?) hated me—to the point that the ceremony was going to be immediate family only with a get-together at Mike's folks' house afterward. And then on the day of the wedding, Paulie's mother, who apparently was seriously crazy, totally freaked out, tried to cut off Paulie's hair while she was getting ready, and then, after somebody managed to get her to take Thorazine to try to calm her down, locked herself in her bedroom until she had to be somewhat forcefully dragged to the ceremony. While the ceremony was going on, Mike and Paulie's friends were all hanging at Mike's parents, buzzing about what other crazy stuff was going on. Just how far would her mother go to stop this from happening? We, of course, smoked a few joints and started getting into some of the food and alcohol that was already laid out for the party. Before we knew it, we had wiped out this six-foot sub sandwich, that was supposed to be the main course for the party, plates full of pastries and cookies from Mike's father's excellent bakery, and almost all the booze. Ooops.

Eventually, the wedding party returned. Mike's parents were stunned at how much of the food and drink we had consumed, but in the context of the day that was a relatively minor problem. Mike and Paulie looked kind of shell-shocked and you could see the rough edges where her mother had cut her hair. But they were married and the party went on.

During his time in Springfield, Mike had found a blue 1963 Ford Econoline van for our trip west. The plan was that right after our wedding, the four of us would drive together out to Oregon. Some mechanic friend of Mike's had checked it out and said it was a good deal for $1,000, so we all chipped in and we had our ride. Sarah and I and a couple of my buddies from Illinois—Swig and Huntsman, who just happened to be cruising the East Coast and showed up for Mike and Paulie's wedding party—drove it back to Philadelphia. Sarah stayed in Philly and the three of us continued on to Illinois, so I could spend some time with my family and Illinois friends before the wedding.

The only problem with the van was that it was a standard shift, a three-speed on the steering wheel column. Despite driving from Boston to San Francisco in Will Poore's stick-shift VW—with great assistance from Will—I still was clunky, at best, with manual shifting.

But Swig and Huntsman were determined to make a man out of me. Like Scotty and Sarah's father and Will before them, their view was that no self-respecting American male should be incapable of working a clutch and hitting the right gears. So as we cruised through the middle of the night on the near-deserted interstate in western Pennsylvania and eastern Ohio, they were my patient tutors.

We pulled into every rest stop along the way, so I would have a chance to practice downshifting and then working my way back up through the gears to get back on the interstate, where I could relax and cruise in third—and just drive, which I *was* awfully damn good at. Every so often they'd have me stop and back into a spot at the rest area, to practice going up to reverse, at the top of the H pattern, unlike the VW, where reverse was off to the left of the H and down—and so they could pee out some of the beer they were steadily consuming as they gently instructed me and cheered me on when I hit a gear smoothly, which didn't happen very often.

I did grind a lot of metal and would still, every once in a while, try to go up the H for first and run into the resistance of reverse. Why was it so hard for me? I was just never a car guy, like a lot of my friends, like just about every American boy growing up in the fifties and sixties. I loved to drive but I didn't really care about how a car worked or what it looked like. I didn't have a biological big brother to teach me that kind of stuff. So my tribal brothers tried.

Finally, somewhere in mid-Ohio as a frigid pastel dawn broke behind us and we made our last stop for gas, we gave up on the instruction and focused on the last couple of hundred miles to our destination. I got through the gears passably to merge onto I-70 west and stayed in third at 75 mph all the way to Urbana, with Swig and Huntsman passed out on the floor behind me. I felt more and more at home in that driver's seat as the day opened before me.

Sarah's cousin's, a rabbi, and my uncle, an Episcopalian minister, performed our wedding ceremony, with some traditional elements—the *huppah* and a smashed glass—mixed with Kahlil Gibran and some of our own poetry recited by our best friends.

Word had spread among our broader range of friends about an open party in Philadelphia and the twenty or twenty-five we had invited to this sit-down dinner, open-bar affair became forty or fifty. Sarah's folks were cool and her dad calmly instructed the bartender to restock the bar after we drank through the original allotment.

It was a wonderful celebration. Freaks in all manner of costumes from torn jeans (Mike) to a frilly, fringy white suit (Walter) danced the *horah* with Sarah's clan of cousins and aunts and uncles from all over Philadelphia and my blue-blooded New England-rooted family. In an era of intense confrontations and seemingly uncrossable cultural chasms, a magical mixing of tribes threaded in sweating and swirling circles, careening into each other with abandon and joy. A dance of a beginning that was also an ending.

Aside from money (about $2,500—another motivation for going through with this wedding thing, if truth be told—it gave us a good stake to start our western adventure), most of our gifts reflected our guests' awareness that we were headed off to a future in a wilderness called Oregon: heavy blankets, warming shawls, survival supplies. North of nowhere, indeed. Stu gave us a dog named Moonbeam, a mix of German shepherd and husky and wolf (!), he said, who was waiting for us in Oregon. She was the sister of his all-white dog, Winter, who he could only get if he took the pair of them. I could easily imagine the smile that crossed his face when he thought up the foolproof way of unloading the second dog—a wedding gift we could hardly refuse.

Throughout the night, Sarah and I drifted now together, now separate, among the gathered crowd, aware that it was the two of us that all this swirled around, the couple now officially sanctioned by gods both Christian and Jewish, by sacraments of alcohol and holy smoke (in not-so-subtle huddles just outside the nearest exterior door), by blessings of parents and siblings and aunts and uncles and cousins named Fairbanks and Shinefeld and Hobson and Katz, by acclamation of friends we'd known since first grade or met in college, played rock and roll and skipped school with, bared our souls to and committed significant proud crimes with. It seemed almost like a spotlight followed each of us around or maybe it was a shining inner light that we were emitting, but we each seemed to glow separately as we circled the room and then the radiance grew brighter as we drew together.

We were married and the night was one great big joyful hallelujah to our union. For all my thinly disguised disdain for the legality and officiousness of the institution, it did change things. In the solemnity of the words, both traditional and stuff we made up, in the legacy of ritual, in the celebratory communal embrace—unconditional for at least these few hours—of our love, our commitment, our shared dreams, I felt a powerful wind propelling us toward a new dimension, a new life as a couple. Husband and wife. Love proclaimed to one and all. Hallelujah and amen!

Unfortunately, that undeniable current could not immediately fix the blue van, the vehicle to our future in Oregon, which had sputtered all the way down from Massachusetts, where I had left it with Mike after the Illinois trip, making Mike and Paulie and Jeffrey and Annie (Jeffrey's new girlfriend; Eddie's former girl friend) and Eddie and Walter late for the proceedings. The van would die whenever it slowed to an idle and then had to be pushed to get started again. Mike waited until near the end of the evening to break the news to us that they had finally pushed it to a nearby parking lot and were not confident it could be started again—even with a push. But even that news could not dampen our rampant joy that night, though somewhere in the back of our minds we knew that meant at least a few days' delay in hitting the road.

So, instead of the blue van, it was the Illinois folks' Sensations mobile that whisked us away from the wedding party, across a couple of parking lots to the Holiday Inn. And, just to finally affirm just how untraditional an affair this was, a half dozen of my buddies from Illinois joined us in our honeymoon "suite" to smoke some of our wedding-present dope and watch us count up our checks.

When they finally left sometime after 2:00 a.m., Sarah and I collapsed on the bed laughing sort of maniacally. Laughing because the pot Walter gave us was pretty damn good, because the Illinois folks had decided to hang out—on our wedding night—after they helped us carry our loot up to the room, because our van was broken and sort of abandoned—this last obstacle only funny after overcoming so many harder ones—because Paulie had brought along her beloved little dog, Quinn Man, who would be joining us on our cross-country trip whenever that did begin, because we now had a part-wolf dog named Moonbeam that we had never met waiting for us, because we really, really, really were going to be together, we really, really, really were married, and we really, really, really were going to Oregon, even though it was put off a bit. Laughing madly because all the waiting and worrying and wondering and waffling and trials were (almost) over. And when we finally stopped laughing, we kissed so slow and deep and long—and it tasted so good. Westward, ho!

ACKNOWLEDGMENTS

Thanks to Cheri Brooks of my former writing group who was never entirely satisfied with the ending of *The Risk of Being Ridiculous*. Here you go, Cheri.

To everyone who lives (fictitiously, of course) in these stories. I hope I got most of it right.

To early readers for their candid wisdom and support: Ross West, Don Marsh, Vern Katz, Bruce Gordon, Joanne Gordon, Kevin Kehoe, Chris Rusch, Larry Weissman, Jim Phelan, Kenny Klein, Jimmy Tarr, Betsy Tarr, Trish Martin, Gale Maynard, Phyllis Maynard, Valerie Maynard, and Peter Newman.

To Gladeye's Jeff Bolkan and Sharleen Nelson for hanging in there with me.

To Al, Judy, Steve, and Jerry Schwartz for letting me in.

To my parents, Guy and Peggy Maynard, for their love and lessons.

To Corey, Jordon, and Jude Maynard, for their love and continuing inspiration.

To Shelley, the hero of all my stories.

Coming late 2024 from GladEye Press

Ash Valley: The Promise of the Land,
the final chapter in the
Risk of Being Ridiculous Trilogy.

Excerpt from Ash Valley …

The TV didn't really even work. Maybe if the wind was blowing just right and the antenna happened to be pointing in the right direction, we might get a fuzzy picture that we could barely make out as channel 5, a CBS station out of Medford. But it was not watchable for any length of time. And besides, well … fuck TV.

It was a spontaneous event. Mike woke up grumpy, saw the blank TV staring back at him as he scowled at the rest of us jammed into the White House "living room" with steaming cups of hobo coffee, "What the fuck is that doing here?" he asked. We all laughed.

"We should put it out of its misery," Dale said. "You know, if you shoot a TV, it implodes."

"What does that even mean?" I asked.

"It just kind of sucks in on itself. Whooooosh!" Dale said as he dramatically spread his hands wide and then drew them together.

"Cool. Do we have a gun?" I asked.

Turns out we did, an Enfield 303 that somebody had given Dale and Sydney. I'm not sure why. Maybe to shoot deer who wandered freely behind the house, in the small flat area—not even really a yard—that quickly gave way to a steep forested rise, which was characteristic of most of the fifty acres that went with the White House. I don't think they had ever actually shot at anything but we had a gun and some bullets and, now, a mission. Dale and I packed the heavy cabinet that contained the TV out over the front porch and loaded it onto the back of Stu's white '52 Chevy pickup. And we all piled in.

A crowd had been waiting for us when Mike and Paulie and Sarah and I first arrived at the White House, jazzed and joyous at the end of our long trek. Jeffrey and Little Eddie and Walter had flown out right after our wedding and some Illinois folks— Huntsman and Swig and Rusty (who'd been with us on the California beaches the previous summer)—somehow beat us there. Tiller fucking Oregon, man, that's where it was happening. The house had five bedrooms but that wasn't even enough. In anticipation of all of us showing up, Dale and Sydney had moved to a cabin on a friend's property further up into the mountains and Stu was staying at another friend's place just a bit upriver from Tiller. Sarah and I, and our new dog, Moonbeam—a sturdy mix of German Shepherd, husky, and, we were told, wolf, who Stu had given us as wedding gift—got a nice big bedroom, the only one on the first floor. Mike and Paulie had the corner bedroom upstairs and Jeffrey had the nicest of the smaller bedrooms. Everybody else just kind of found a spot in the other rooms. It was apparent from the start that, as perfect as the White House sounded when there were just four or five people living there and the rest of us were dreaming of escapes from apartments in the city, it was not going to work as our long-term home, not enough living space, not enough farmable land. But it was a good landing spot, a base where we could orient ourselves and look for the right place …

We dove right into getting stuff done. We sold the van for $1,115 ($65 more than we paid for it—not counting the $175 we had to pay to fix it in Philly), planning to replace it with a pick-up, hoping to buy one from the same guy who sold Stu his, an old man named Earl who lived a ways downriver and had taken a liking to our band of refugees from the East.

Paulie already had her eyes on a horse, her first Oregon dream, a ten-year-old gelding named Stormy. Sarah and I were going to chip in and the horse would belong to the group, but we all knew that it would mainly be Paulie's horse. Sometimes it seemed Paulie connected with animals better than she did with people. When we had to stay at Sarah's parent's house one more night after the van was fixed after the wedding, Quinn Man had to sleep in the van because the Stein's two dogs were not receptive to him hanging out in the house. Paulie opted to sleep in the van with him, rather than with Mike in the house. Soon, she would have a horse. At first, she would keep him at a stable on the place where Stu was staying with a guy named Stephen, who was renting a cabin from a mother-and-daughter family on their place a few miles upriver.

Sarah and Jeffrey and I spent part of a day working in a small garden plot next to the driveway in front of the house. The dirt was still somewhat wet from all the spring rains, but we had a few sunny days when the temperatures got up into the sixties and the soil dried just enough to be workable. We were anxious, too, to do anything that seemed to move us toward this new life we had imagined. Man, it felt good to get that good moist Oregon dirt between our fingers, to get dirty even if we didn't really know what we were doing. On Stu's direction, we covered the fresh-tilled ground with some hay, to keep it from turning to mud in the next rain and to, eventually, add some nutrients. Our next step was to plant some tomato starts in pots and get some posts for a fence to keep the ever-present deer out.

After working up a sweat in the garden, Sarah and I walked across the road to the river. The brush was thick on the short steep bank, but a narrow path, twelve or fifteen feet long, led to a small natural gravel beach, where we could stretch out and soak in the powerful afternoon sun.

I had never really experienced the roar of a river up close. My childhood home of New Bedford, Massachusetts, was at the mouth of the Acushnet River. But I never knew it as a river. In my limited scope, that river was what went under the bridge to Fairhaven, just at the edge of the harbor, which opened on to Buzzards Bay, which was an extension of the Atlantic Ocean. The ocean, with its waves and tides and rhythmic rumble and vast horizons, was the water I knew, the water that mattered. In my Illinois teen years, the plodding brown rivers, which I took scant notice of, seemed no more than drainage ditches with names. One notable exception to my lack of awareness was a hot summer night when Scottie and I, after a band gig in Dubuque, Iowa, joined a party of strangers on the Mississippi River, floating easily in slow murky warm water with cold beers in our hand, a blissful sort of scene until we were attacked by a gang of unfriendly local greasers and had to escape through dense bankside brush followed by a long slog along railroad tracks, stranded 250 miles from home. That river, it turned out, was no joyful glide but a lazy, dirty, dangerous trap.

When I went back to Massachusetts for college, I landed next to the Charles River. It, too, seemed slow, but much more civilized than the northern Mississippi, with sailboats and rowers in sleek sculls and carefully cultivated paths along its banks. In my early days there, lonely and lost in a new place with no friends, the easy flow of the river was soothing, a welcome contrast to the urban hubbub just steps away and the constant clamor in my head. Walking the Charles had a certain philosophical weight, I thought, and in my first college days, I imagined I was destined to be a deep thinker. Walking beside the river with my hands studiously clasped behind my back seemed part of living that role. Long after those fantasies of intellectual prowess had been exploded by pot and LSD and friends who humbled me, Sarah and I got to know each other walking along the Charles, about two-thirds of the way through our freshman year. I was deeply attracted to her, but she was just looking for a sympathetic somebody to talk to about troubles with her Philadelphia boyfriend and how she fit into the tribe of freaks and radicals that our group of friends was becoming, the tribe that eventually would emigrate to Tiller, Oregon.

We'd slip away from the near constant party in our dorms, navigate the grimy underside of the Mass Pike, dart daringly across Storrow Drive, and there we were on the tree-lined banks of the Charles. The more we talked, the more attracted I became to her, to her fundamental honesty, her natural empathy, her no-bullshit intellect—and the more I listened, the more I became the trusted friend, the safe not-boyfriend. It was an agonizing dilemma for me for quite a while. But it was, I believe, those thoughtful walks along that wide quiet river when I had little hope that showed her some part of me that eventually she thought she could love. There must have been some deep vibes beyond my understanding in the flow of that river.

But the Charles never roared. The South Umpqua, loaded from spring rains and snowmelt, powered by its rapid descent from the Cascade peaks that rose to the east of us, positively roared—a roar that was a song, a soliloquy, and a symphony, a single powerful voice and glorious universal chorus. Hesse, I think, once wrote that all the sounds of the world could be heard in the river's music if only we learned to listen better.

I heard majesty and power as I lay in awe on the warm fine gravel next to Sarah, a welcome and a warning. This was the song of our new world, the mighty green trees a short stone's toss away on the other side, the deep blue sky emerging from fleeting gray clouds above us, the gray-blue mountain water rushing white over exposed boulders and scattered remnants of logs.

We shed our clothes and waded in gingerly through the shifty gravel and around sharp rocks. The water was fucking freezing. Sarah stopped when the water reached her thigh, balancing against the current, holding her arms across her pale white chest, laughing and grimacing at the same time—Sarah, naked in the South Umpqua River, sparkling with fresh wetness, framed by Oregon's raw splendor, beautiful in an entirely new way. I moved a little further out until it was just deep enough for me to drop down and immerse my whole body in the river. A baptism. Shocked by cold, I jump to my feet as fast as I could in the slippery footing, and screamed as loud as I could: "Wooooooooooh, ooooh, ooo." As thrilled as I was chilled to the bone.

I lunged toward Sarah still shivering in the shallows and before she could put up any defense, I had her in my arms, wetting her with the river water that dripped from me. We kissed deep and quick, completing the ceremony, then hurried to the warmth of the dry gravel. I was deliriously happy.

We presented quite a scene heading to the dump in Stu's pick-up. We, of course, had gotten good and stoned before we left the White House. Most of us piled in the back around the condemned TV. Stu drove, with Paulie in the middle and Mike riding shotgun. Mike carried the rifle and occasionally would brandish it out the window to clenched-fist cheers and laughter from those of us in the back, and Dale and Sidney, following behind in their VW bus, would honk their horn. A merry band of revolutionaries we were.

We ceremoniously hauled the TV off the truck bed and placed it on the edge of the parking area, the lip overlooking the dump's pit. We had the dump to ourselves. Mike still had the gun. It seemed only right that he would be the executioner. We lined up loosely behind him as he knelt and brought the rifle to his shoulder.

It was a goof, this ritualistic killing, just a fun way to get rid of a broken-down old TV. But, man, what would be a better way to declare our independence from all we had left behind, consumerism and lowest common denominator entertainment, false values and brainwashing, a society so convinced that it was the greatest fucking thing the world had ever seen that it had lost the ability to think critically about itself. McLuhan had told us that television had laid the groundwork for the cultural revolution, that, as a "hot" medium, it taught us to expect to have some control over our lives and our world. Maybe there's some truth to that. There was no doubt that watching the events around the Kennedy assassination and almost live coverage of the war in Vietnam and the riots in the inner cities and the Chicago cops gone berserk at the '68 Democratic National Convention had made deep imprints on our consciousness. But television was also the ultimate expression of the vacuous materialism that we were trying to escape. We had to kill it.

At the Tiller dump, nobody gave any speeches or deep analysis. Mike made one shot to dead center, and then we all heard the eerie "Whooooooooooooosh" as the shattered screen sucked in on itself. It was quiet for a few beats as we all looked around wide-eyed at each other and then somebody said, "Far fucking out," and we rushed to kick the carcass down into the pit.

ABOUT THE AUTHOR

 Guy Maynard lived in New Bedford, Massachusetts for his first thirteen years. He spent his high school years in Urbana, Illinois, and went to two years of college in Boston. He was lead singer in a teen rock and roll band, was active in the civil rights and anti–Vietnam War movements, worked as a carpenter, and was a member of a worker-owned construction company.

After receiving his degree in journalism from the University of Oregon in 1984, he was editor of a small community newspaper and then worked on a number of trade magazines in fields such as liquid and gas chromatography and geographic information systems. He was editor of *Oregon Quarterly*, the University of Oregon magazine, for seventeen years. He was editor of *The Elements of Building* (by Mark Q. Kerson) and *How to Build a Conestoga Hut* (by Erik de Buhr) and was co-editor of the 2003 collection, *Best Essays NW*. His essays and articles have appeared in numerous newspapers, magazines, and books. *Trial* is his second novel.

Visit https://www.facebook.com/TheRiskofBeingRidiculous

MORE BOOKS FROM GLADEYE PRESS

The Time Tourists
The Yesterday Girl
Sharleen Nelson

Follow the adventures and missteps of time-traveling PI Imogen Oliver as she recovers lost items and unearths long-buried stories and secrets from the past in this exciting series!

The Fragile Blue Dot
Ross West

Veteran science-writer and journalist Ross West's collection of award-winning short fiction touches on the human aspect of living in a world on the brink of ecological disaster.

Dye. Run. Don't Die: A Love Story
K.G. Kolsen

Chased by shadowy figures, Winnie and Jimmy reunite somewhere between Oklahoma and Colorado and embark on a wild ride filled with disguises, stolen vehicles, murders, truck-stop perverts, a sex-cult, deadly shootouts, and rediscovered love.

The Risk of Being Ridiculous
Guy Maynard

Join 19-year-old Ben Tucker for a passionate, lyrical six-week ride through confrontation and confusion, courts and cops, parties and politics, school and the streets, Weathermen and women's liberation, acid and activism, revolution and reaction.

All GladEye titles are available for purchase at
www.gladeyepress.com and your local bookstore.

Federation of the Dragon
Footman of the Ether
Jason A. Kilgore
Enter the ancient world of Irikara for
high-stakes epic fantasy adventure
in a mythical land filled with dragons
and demons, dwarves and elves,
magic and mages and gods.

The Midnight Show: bohemians, byways, and bonfires
Camille Cole
During the early days of Oregon's famous Country
Fair, the Midnight Show was a stage shared by
icons of the counterculture, lovers, children and
family, and those of us finding our way through.

Tripping the Field: An Existential Crisis of Ungodly Proportions
Ian Jaydid
Empiricist scientist, Prof. Michael Huxley, tumbles,
stumbles, strides and crawls through the jungles
of South America, the mountains of Tibet, and the
backwoods of Colorado in search of enlightenment
and the hope of saving the world from a religious cult
that has discovered a dark shortcut to the power of
quantum realities.

A Recipe for Dying
Patricia Brown
The old people are dying in the small coastal town of
Waterton, but no one seems to notice—after all,
that's what old folk do, isn't it? Eleanor and her de-
lightful assortment of friends, most whom are getting
up in age, set out to discover what is going on. Is it a
series of mercy killings, or murder, and is their
investigation putting them in danger?

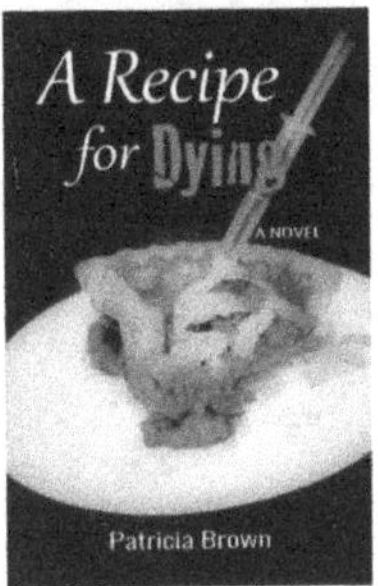

COMING late 2024 *from*

Ash Valley
Guy Maynard
In this final installment in the trilogy, Ben Tucker, his soulmate Sarah, and a community of like-minded friends forge new bonds while seeking peace and tranquility far away from Boston at a commune in the rugged Pacific Northwest.

The End of Time
Sharleen Nelson
Book three in this exciting series follows the continuing adventures of time-traveling private investigator Imogen Oliver as she uncovers shocking new revelations about her family, faces more challenges in her rocky relationships, and the threat of a power-hungry villain who wants to shut down time travel for good.